SPOOKY
CAMPFIRE
STORIES

SPOOKY CAMPFIRE STORIES

Outdoor Myths and Tales for All Ages

Second Edition

Edited by Amy Kelley Hoitsma

FALCONGUIDES

GUILFORD, CONNECTICUT
HELENA, MONTANA
AN IMPRINT OF **ROWMAN & LITTLEFIELD**

FALCONGUIDES®

Copyright © 2012 by Rowman & Littlefield
Previously published by Falcon Publishing, Inc.

FalconGuides is an imprint of Rowman & Littlefield

Falcon, FalconGuides, and Outfit Your Mind are registered trademarks of Rowman & Littlefield.

Grateful acknowledgment is made to those who granted permission to reprint the selections in this book. A complete list of copyright permissions begins on page 133.

Library of Congress Cataloging-in-Publication Data
Spooky campfire stories : outdoor myths and tales for all ages / edited by Amy Kelley Hoitsma. — 2nd ed.
    v. cm.
  Contents: The tell-tale heart / Edgar Allan Poe — The boarded window / Ambrose Bierce — From Faces at the window / Rose Wilder Lane — He walked by day / Julius Long — The wendigo / Alvin Schwartz — The severed hand / Janice M. Del Negro — Knock, knock, who's there? / J.J. Reneaux — Ma Yarwood's wedding ring / Rita Cox — Home / Shirley Jackson — One chance / Ethel Helene Coen — The fly / Arthur Porges — To build a fire / Jack London.
  ISBN 978-0-7627-7804-1
  1. Ghost stories, American. 2. Horror tales, American. [1. Horror stories. 2. Short stories.] I. Hoitsma, Amy Kelley.
  PZ5.S757 2012
  [Fic]—dc23

                                                    2011032697

Printed in the United States of America
Distributed by NATIONAL BOOK NETWORK

CONTENTS

INTRODUCTION

Who doesn't love a good ghost story when sitting around a campfire with friends or family on a warm summer night?

The dinner dishes are done, there's no TV or computer. The evening's entertainment is up to you. You pull out a book—perhaps hold a flashlight under your chin for that glowing-head effect—and begin to read aloud, hamming it up with creepy voices and sound effects. Suddenly the fire pops! And your listeners practically jump out of their skin! Everyone laughs, but secretly they're feeling slightly on edge and no longer looking forward to zipping themselves into a dark tent. . . .

It takes me back to my own childhood, on the semiannual family camping trip to northern Wisconsin (how did we fit seven people in one tent?), or at a slumber party where the true goal was not to sleep at all. A good, creepy tale or urban murder myth was an essential ingredient to a memorable night.

I put the first edition of this anthology together ten years ago. It's been fun to reread the stories I chose then and to have the chance to switch out a few with some new ones. There's a wide range of stories here, so you should be able to find something to fit your audience. There are several classics, including stories by the great Edgar Allan Poe, Ambrose Bierce—a master at the ghost-story "punch line"—and Jack London ("To Build a Fire" was first read to me on an afternoon boat trip, and I still remember feeling a distinct chill and panic set in despite the blazing July sun). Several stories—such as "Knock Knock, Who's There?"—are regional tales, passed on from one generation to the next through storytelling. And one story will cause you to think twice about swatting a housefly ever again! That said, I don't think any of the selections are too scary for younger readers and listeners or too long to read aloud in an evening.

If I have one wish for this book, it's that these stories be read aloud, so that both reader and listener can indulge in the simple pleasures that storytelling brings.

And have a good night's sleep!

THE TELL-TALE HEART

Edgar Allan Poe

TRUE!—nervous—very, very dreadfully nervous I had been and am; but why *will* you say that I am mad? The disease had sharpened my senses—not destroyed—not dulled them. Above all was the sense of hearing acute. I heard all things in the heaven and in the earth. I heard many things in hell. How, then, am I mad? Hearken! and observe how healthily—how calmly I can tell you the whole story.

It is impossible to say how first the idea entered my brain; but once conceived, it haunted me day and night. Object there was none. Passion there was none. I loved the old man. He had never wronged me. He had never given me insult. For his gold I had no desire. I think it was his eye! yes, it was this! One of his eyes resembled that of a vulture—a pale blue eye, with a film over it. Whenever it fell upon me, my blood ran cold; and so by degrees—very gradually—I made up my mind to take the life of the old man, and thus rid myself of the eye for ever.

Now this is the point. You fancy me mad. Madmen know nothing. But you should have seen *me*. You should have seen how wisely I proceeded—with what caution—with what foresight—with what dissimulation I went to work! I was never kinder to the old man than during the whole week before I killed him. And every night, about midnight, I turned the latch of his door and opened it—oh, so gently! And then, when I had made an opening sufficient for my head, I put in a dark lantern, all closed, closed, so that no light shone out, and then I thrust in my head. Oh, you would have laughed to see how cunningly I thrust it in! I moved it slowly—very, very slowly, so that I might not disturb the old man's sleep. It took me an hour to place my whole head within the opening so far that I could see him as he lay upon his bed. Ha!—would a madman have been so wise as this? And then, when my head was well in the room, I undid the lantern cautiously—oh, so cautiously—cautiously (for the hinges creaked)—I undid it just so much that a single thin ray fell upon the vulture eye. And this I did for seven long nights—every night just at midnight—but I found the eye always closed; and so it was impossible to do the work; for it was not the old man who vexed me, but his Evil Eye. And every morning, when the day broke, I went boldly into the chamber, and spoke courageously to him, calling him by name in a hearty tone, and inquiring how he had passed the night. So you see he would have been a very profound old man, indeed, to suspect that every night, just at twelve, I looked in upon him while he slept.

Upon the eighth night I was more than usually cautious in opening the door. A watch's minute hand moves more quickly than did mine. Never before that night had I *felt* the extent of my own powers—of my sagacity. I could scarcely contain my feelings of triumph. To think that there I was, opening the door, little by little, and he not even to dream of my secret deeds or thoughts. I fairly chuckled at the idea; and perhaps he heard me; for he moved on the bed suddenly, as if startled. Now you may think that I drew back—but no. His room was as black as pitch with the thick darkness (for the shutters were close fastened, through fear of robbers), and so I knew that he could not see the opening of the door, and I kept pushing it on steadily, steadily.

I had my head in, and was about to open the lantern, when my thumb slipped upon the tin fastening, and the old man sprang up in the bed, crying out—"Who's there?"

I kept quite still and said nothing. For a whole hour I did not move a muscle, and in the meantime I did not hear him lie down. He was still sitting up in the bed listening—just as I have done, night after night, hearkening to the death watches in the wall.

Presently I heard a slight groan, and I knew it was the groan of mortal terror. It was not a groan of pain or of grief—oh, no!—it was the low stifled sound that arises from the bottom of the soul when overcharged with awe. I knew the sound well. Many a night, just at midnight, when all the world slept, it has welled up from my own bosom, deepening, with its dreadful echo, the terrors that distracted me. I say I knew it well. I knew what the old man felt, and pitied him, although I chuckled at heart. I knew that he had been lying awake ever since the first slight noise, when he had turned in the bed. His fears had been ever since growing upon him. He had been trying to fancy them causeless, but could not. He had been saying to himself—"It is nothing but the wind in the chimney—it is only a mouse crossing the floor,"or "it is merely a cricket which has made a single chirp." Yes, he had been trying to comfort himself with these suppositions; but he had found all in vain. *All in vain;* because Death, in approaching him, had stalked with his black shadow before him, and enveloped the victim. And it was the mournful influence of the unperceived shadow that caused him to feel—although he neither saw nor heard—to *feel* the presence of my head within the room.

When I had waited a long time, very patiently, without hearing him lie down, I resolved to open a little—a very, very little crevice in the lantern. So I opened it—you cannot imagine how stealthily, stealthily—until, at length, a single dim ray, like the thread of the spider, shot from out the crevice and fell upon the vulture eye.

It was open—wide, wide open—and I grew furious as I gazed upon it. I saw it with perfect distinctness—all a dull blue, with a hideous veil over it that chilled the very marrow in my bones; but I could see nothing else of the old man's face or person: for I had directed the ray as if by instinct, precisely upon the damned spot.

And now have I not told you that what you mistake for madness is but over-acuteness of the senses?—now, I say, there came to my ears a low, dull, quick sound, such as a watch makes when enveloped in cotton. I knew *that* sound well too. It was the beating of the old man's heart. It increased my fury, as the beating of a drum stimulates the soldier into courage.

But even yet I refrained and kept still. I scarcely breathed. I held the lantern motionless. I tried how steadily I could maintain the ray upon the eye. Meantime the hellish tattoo of the heart increased. It grew quicker and quicker, and louder and louder every instant. The old man's terror must have been extreme! It grew louder, I say, louder every moment!—do you mark me well? I have told you that I am nervous: so I am. And now at the dead hour of the night, amid the dreadful silence of that old house, so strange a noise as this excited me to uncontrollable terror. Yet, for some minutes longer I refrained and stood still. But the beating grew louder, louder! I thought the heart must burst. And now a new anxiety seized me—the sound would be heard by a neighbor! The old man's hour had come! With a loud yell, I threw open the lantern and leaped into the room. He shrieked once—once only. In an instant I dragged him to the floor, and pulled the heavy bed over him. I then smiled gaily, to find the deed so far done. But, for many minutes, the heart beat on with a muffled sound. This, however, did not vex me; it would not be heard through the wall. At length it ceased. The old man was dead. I removed the bed and examined the corpse. Yes, he was stone, stone dead. I placed my hand upon the heart and held it there many minutes. There was no pulsation. He was stone dead. His eye would trouble me no more.

If still you think me mad, you will think so no longer when I describe the wise precautions I took for the concealment of the body. The night waned, and I worked hastily, but in silence. First of all I dismembered the corpse. I cut off the head and the arms and the legs.

I then took up three planks from the flooring of the chamber, and deposited all between the scantlings. I then replaced the boards so cleverly, so cunningly, that no human eye—not even *his*—could have detected any thing wrong. There was nothing to wash out—no stain of any kind—no blood-spot whatever. I had been too wary for that. A tub had caught all—ha! ha!

When I had made an end of these labors, it was four o'clock—still dark as midnight. As the bell sounded the hour, there came a knocking at the street door. I went down to open it with a light heart—for what had I *now* to fear? There entered three men, who introduced themselves, with perfect suavity, as officers of the police. A shriek had been heard by a neighbor during the night; suspicion of foul play had been aroused; information had been lodged at the police office, and they (the officers) had been deputed to search the premises.

I smiled—for *what* had I to fear? I bade the gentlemen welcome. The shriek, I said, was my own in a dream. The old man, I mentioned, was absent in the country. I took my visitors all over the house. I bade them search—search *well*. I led them, at length, to *his* chamber. I showed them his treasures, secure, undisturbed. In the enthusiasm of my confidence, I brought chairs into the room, and desired them *here* to rest from their fatigues, while I myself, in the wild audacity of my perfect triumph, placed my own seat upon the very spot beneath which reposed the corpse of the victim.

The officers were satisfied. My *manner* had convinced them. I was singularly at ease. They sat, and while I answered cheerily, they chatted familiar things. But, ere long, I felt myself getting pale and wished them gone. My head ached, and I fancied a ringing in my ears:

but still they sat and still chatted. The ringing became more distinct—it continued and became more distinct: I talked more freely to get rid of the feeling: but it continued and gained definitiveness—until, at length, I found that the noise was *not* within my ears.

No doubt I now grew *very* pale; but I talked more fluently, and with a heightened voice. Yet the sound increased—and what could I do? It was a *low, dull, quick sound—much such a sound as a watch makes when enveloped in cotton.* I gasped for breath—and yet the officers heard it not. I talked more quickly—more vehemently; but the noise steadily increased. I arose and argued about trifles, in a high key and with violent gesticulations, but the noise steadily increased. Why *would* they not be gone? I paced the floor to and fro with heavy strides, as if excited to fury by the observation of the men—but the noise steadily increased. Oh God! what *could* I do? I foamed—I raved—I swore! I swung the chair upon which I had been sitting, and grated it upon the boards, but the noise arose over all and continually increased. It grew louder—louder—*louder!* And still the men chatted pleasantly, and smiled. Was it possible they heard not? Almighty God!—no, no! They heard—they suspected!—they *knew!*—they were making a mockery of my horror!—this I thought, and this I think. But anything was better than this agony! Any thing was more tolerable than this derision! I could bear those hypocritical smiles no longer! I felt that I must scream or die!—and now—again!—hark! louder! louder! louder! *louder!*

"Villains!" I shrieked, "dissemble no more! I admit the deed!—tear up the planks!—here, here!—it is the beating of his hideous heart!"

THE BOARDED WINDOW

Ambrose Bierce

In 1830, only a few miles away from what is now the great city of Cincinnati, lay an immense and almost unbroken forest. The whole region was sparsely settled by people of the frontier—restless souls who no sooner had hewn fairly habitable homes out of the wilderness and attained to that degree of prosperity which today we should call indigence than impelled by some mysterious impulse of their nature they abandoned all and pushed farther westward, to encounter new perils and privations in the effort to regain the meagre comforts which they had voluntarily renounced. Many of them had already forsaken that region for the remoter settlements, but among those remaining was one who had been of those first arriving. He lived alone in a house of logs surrounded on all sides by the great forest, of whose gloom and silence he seemed a part, for no one had ever known him to smile nor speak a needless word. His simple wants were supplied by the sale or barter of skins of wild animals in the river town, for not a thing did he grow upon the land which, if needful, he might have claimed by right of undisturbed possession. There were evidences of "improvement"— a few acres of ground immediately about the house had once been cleared of its trees, the decayed stumps of which were half concealed by the new growth that had been suffered to repair the ravage wrought by the ax. Apparently the man's zeal for agriculture had burned with a failing flame, expiring in penitential ashes.

The little log house, with its chimney of sticks, its roof of warping clapboards weighted with traversing poles and its "chinking" of clay, had a single door and, directly opposite, a window. The latter, however, was boarded up— nobody could remember a time when it was not. And none knew why it was so closed; certainly not because of the occupant's dislike of light and air, for on those rare occasions when a hunter had passed that lonely spot the recluse had commonly been seen sunning himself on his doorstep if heaven had provided sunshine for his need. I fancy there are few persons living today who ever knew the secret of that window, but I am one, as you shall see.

The man's name was said to be Murlock. He was apparently seventy years old, actually about fifty. Something besides years had had a hand in his aging. His hair and long, full beard were white, his gray, lustreless eyes sunken, his face singularly seamed with wrinkles which appeared to belong to two intersecting systems. In figure he was tall and spare, with a stoop of the shoulders—a burden bearer. I never saw him; these particulars I learned from my grandfather, from whom also I got the man's story when I was a lad. He had known him when living near by in that early day.

One day Murlock was found in his cabin, dead. It was not a time and place for coroners and newspapers, and I suppose it was agreed that he had died from natural causes or I should have been told, and should remember. I know only that with what was probably a sense of the fitness of things the body was buried near the cabin, alongside the grave of his wife, who had preceded him by so many years that local tradition had retained hardly a hint of her existence. That closes the final chapter of this true story—excepting, indeed, the circumstance that many years afterward, in company with an equally intrepid spirit, I penetrated to the place and ventured near enough to the ruined cabin to throw a stone against it, and ran away to avoid the ghost which every well-informed boy thereabout knew haunted the spot. But there is an earlier chapter—that supplied by my grandfather.

When Murlock built his cabin and began laying sturdily about with his ax to hew out a farm—the rifle, meanwhile, his means of support—he was young, strong and full of hope. In that eastern country whence he came he had married, as was the fashion, a young woman in all ways worthy of his honest devotion, who shared the dangers and privations of his lot with a willing spirit and light heart. There is no known record of her name; of her charms of mind and person tradition is silent and the doubter is at liberty to entertain his doubt; but God forbid that I should share it! Of their affection and happiness there is abundant assurance in every added day of the man's widowed life; for what but the magnetism of a blessed memory could have chained that venturesome spirit to a lot like that?

One day Murlock returned from gunning in a distant part of the forest to find his wife prostrate with fever, and delirious. There was no physician within miles, no neighbor; nor was she in a condition to be left, to summon help. So he set about the task of nursing her back to health, but at the end of the third day she fell into unconsciousness and so passed away, apparently, with never a gleam of returning reason.

From what we know of a nature like his we may venture to sketch in some of the details of the outline picture drawn by my grandfather. When convinced that she was dead, Murlock had sense enough to remember that the dead must be prepared for burial. In performance of this sacred duty he blundered now and again, did certain things incorrectly, and others which he did correctly were done over and over. His occasional failures to accomplish some simple and ordinary act filled him with astonishment, like that of a drunken man who wonders at the suspension of familiar natural laws. He was surprised, too, that he did not weep—surprised and a little ashamed; surely it is unkind not to weep for the dead. "Tomorrow," he said aloud, "I shall have to make the coffin and dig the grave; and then I shall miss her, when she is no longer in sight; but now—she is dead, of course, but it is all right—it must be all right, somehow. Things cannot be so bad as they seem."

He stood over the body in the fading light, adjusting the hair and putting the finishing touches to the simple toilet, doing all mechanically, with soulless care. And still through his consciousness ran an undersense of conviction that all was right—that he should have her again as before, and everything explained. He had had no experience in grief; his capacity had not been enlarged by use. His heart could not contain it all, nor his imagination rightly conceive it. He did not know he was so hard struck; that knowledge would come later, and never go. Grief is an artist of powers as various as the instruments upon which he plays his dirges for the dead, evoking from some the sharpest, shrillest notes, from others the low, grave chords that throb recurrent like the slow beating of a distant drum. Some natures it startles; some it stupefies. To one it comes like the stroke of an arrow, stinging all the sensibilities to a keener life; to another as the blow of a bludgeon, which in crushing benumbs. We may conceive Murlock to have been that way affected, for (and here we are upon surer ground than that of conjecture) no sooner had he finished his pious work than, sinking into a chair by the side of the table upon which the body lay, and noting how white the profile showed in the deepening gloom, he laid his arms upon the table's edge, and dropped his face into them, tearless yet and unutterably weary. At that moment came in through the open window a long, wailing sound like the cry of a lost child in the far deeps of the darkening wood! But the man did not move. Again, and nearer than before, sounded that unearthly cry upon his failing sense. Perhaps it was a wild beast; perhaps it was a dream. For Murlock was asleep.

Some hours later, as it afterward appeared, this unfaithful watcher awoke and lifting his head from his arms intently listened—he knew not why. There in the black darkness by the side of the dead, recalling all without a shock, he strained his eyes to see—he knew not what. His senses were all alert, his breath was suspended, his blood had stilled its tides as if to assist the silence. Who—what had waked him, and where was it?

Suddenly the table shook beneath his arms, and at the same moment he heard, or fancied that he heard, a light, soft step—another—sounds as of bare feet upon the floor!

He was terrified beyond the power to cry out or move. Perforce he waited—waited there in the darkness through seeming centuries of such dread as one may know, yet live to tell. He tried vainly to speak the dead woman's name, vainly to stretch forth his hand across the table to learn if she were there. His throat was powerless, his arms and hands were like lead. Then occurred something most frightful. Some heavy body seemed hurled against the table with an impetus that pushed it against his breast so sharply as nearly to overthrow him, and at the same instant he heard and felt the fall of something upon the floor with so violent a thump that the whole house was shaken by the impact. A scuffling ensued, and a confusion of sounds impossible to describe. Murlock had risen to his feet. Fear had by excess forfeited control of his faculties. He flung his hands upon the table. Nothing was there!

There is a point at which terror may turn to madness; and madness incites to action. With no definite intent, from no motive but the wayward impulse of a madman, Murlock sprang to the wall, with a little groping seized his loaded rifle, and without aim discharged it. By the flash which lit up the room with a vivid illumination, he saw an enormous panther dragging the dead woman toward the window, its teeth fixed in her throat! Then there were darkness blacker than before, and silence; and when he returned to consciousness the sun was high and the wood vocal with songs of birds.

The body lay near the window, where the beast had left it when frightened away by the flash and report of the rifle. The clothing was deranged, the long hair in disorder, the limbs lay anyhow. From the throat, dreadfully lacerated, had issued a pool of blood not yet entirely coagulated. The ribbon with which he had bound the wrists was broken; the hands were tightly clenched. Between the teeth was a fragment of the animal's ear.

FACES AT THE WINDOW

Rose Wilder Lane

In the white glare of light and the faint oily odor of hot hair, Gladys told me the enthralling story of her life.

She was next to the youngest of thirteen children, and all alone in the world. Where her twelve brothers and sisters were, she had no idea at all; she had not seen nor heard of any of them since she was eight years old, because then her mother died and her father just went away. They did not know what to do, and sort of scattered. I had the impression of a nestful of little quails, scattered and cowering in the grass without a mother. Gladys stayed with a neighbor for a while but they made her work too hard, so she left there. She walked into Memphis, where a policeman took her to a

21

police station and some people wanted to put her in an orphan asylum, but she got away from them. She went to back doors asking for work, and she had worked a year for a nice woman who had three little children and gave her some clothes. But then there was yellow fever in Memphis and so many people died that everyone left Memphis that could. That nice family left, and Gladys was scared of yellow fever, so she left Memphis, too.

When she was fourteen years old, but she said she was fifteen, she was clerking in a bookstore in Colorado Springs. It was easy, clean work and she liked it; $3 a week and they let her read the magazines. There she met a girl named Amy, who came in to buy books. Amy was fourteen and she was an only child. She was in Colorado for her health; she had consumption and she was living in a hotel with her parents until she got well. Gladys and Amy became great friends; they were together all the time and Amy's parents were pleased because Amy was so much happier, she was always laughing when she was with Gladys; they had such good times! Gladys was almost one of the family. Then Amy got well, and they were taking her back home to Mayfield, Kentucky, so she and Gladys had to part.

Gladys felt bad about it, but not as bad as Amy. Amy cried and cried, she said she'd die without Gladys; they couldn't get her to stop crying and sure enough, she cried herself so sick that they had to call the doctor again. The doctor advised them not to take her away from Gladys. So her father and mother talked to Gladys and said she was all alone in the world, there was nothing to keep her in Colorado Springs, and if she would come with them they would sort of adopt her as a sister to Amy and she could live with them like one of the family as long as she wanted to, or for always if she wanted to. And she did want to. This was the most wonderful thing that ever happened to her in her whole life.

I remember Gladys' face when she said that; she meant it. Nothing else so wonderful had happened to her in her life, and it had not happened. For here she was in the Midland Hotel in Kansas City, a Postal branch-office operator earning $30 a month and living, as I knew, in a $2-a-week hall bedroom in a rooming house. What happened? I wanted eagerly to know.

Well, Gladys said, it was queer; it was very queer and she did not understand it at all, and maybe I wouldn't believe it, but it was so; cross her heart and hope to die, it was the honest truth. They went to Mayfield, Kentucky. They traveled in the sleeping cars; Gladys slept in a Pullman berth, and ate in a dining car. Maybe they weren't exactly rich, not as rich as Rockefeller and people like that, but they did have a lot of money and Gladys's keep was no burden to them. When they got to Mayfield, at first they had a hard time finding a place to live. Amy's father owned a business there, but they had sold their house when they went to Colorado for Amy's health, not knowing how long they would be gone. Now Mayfield was growing fast; the hotel was full, all the nice places were rented, and they had to buy or build a new house. That would take some time. So meanwhile they rented what they could get, and it was an old house, not even painted, right on the bank of the river. They rented it by the month, till they could get into their new home.

It was a big house, bare and sort of echoing inside. They didn't really furnish it; their furniture was in storage and they only took out a few things like beds and some chairs and lamps, and a stove and table in the kitchen, because they were only camping there till the new house was ready. The first thing that happened was, in the middle of the first night, every one of them had the most frightful nightmare. They were all so scared that they got up and lighted lamps, and at midnight they were all together in the kitchen. They made some coffee and drank it and stayed there till daylight.

The next night, exactly the same thing happened. They were all in the kitchen again, all scared by nightmares. In the daytime, it seemed so silly to act that way for nothing but a bad dream, probably from something you'd eaten or maybe because you were sleeping in a strange place, and you were so tired you were sure you'd sleep tonight. They'd all be laughing at each other for yawning, and right after supper, as soon as Amy and Gladys did the supper dishes, they all went to bed and sound asleep. Then in the middle of the night it happened again; they'd wake up screaming, and light lamps, and all get together in the kitchen. The queer thing was, not one of them could remember what they'd dreamed. At first Amy's father wouldn't let them talk about it; but now, when they did, they could not remember what they had dreamed that scared them so.

Amy's mother said probably it came from drinking so much coffee, in the middle of the night too, so she made cocoa. They all agreed that they'd have a nice cup of cocoa and then go back to bed, but they didn't; they just sat there in the lamplight till morning. Every morning the whole thing seemed so silly and everything was all right all day, and then at night the same thing happened again.

Gladys said she supposed you got used to almost anything in time, and after a couple of weeks they were sort of used to having those awful nightmares and anyway she was too sleepy to care much, but then they saw the faces. They were not real faces, they couldn't be, but whether I believed it or not, she saw them. They all saw those faces. At least, Amy said she did, her father and mother said they did, and Gladys knew she did. She would swear it on the Bible.

When they went in the kitchen, in the night, with the lamp lighted and it was black night outside, they saw those faces looking in through the kitchen window. You know how sometimes you see your face reflected in a window pane? These faces were like that, but they were not reflections of anyone inside the kitchen. They were faces of old men, and young men, and women and boys and girls. Different faces, sometimes a crowd of them, and then only one.

Amy's father said they were all worn out and imagining things; he said there was nobody outside that window. They all knew there was nobody there; there couldn't be because the kitchen wall was at the very edge of the river bank. The bank went straight down to the river below, and outside that window there wasn't ground enough for anyone to stand on.

Next day Amy's father put a window-shade on that window. He said that nothing was hurting them; they were only imagining things that weren't so, and he had bought another house; they would move into it six weeks later, when the owner had agreed to move out. Gladys had looked out of the upstairs window and made sure that nobody could possibly stand outside the kitchen window looking in. That afternoon, before sunset, Amy's mother pulled down the shade. Nothing happened that night but the nightmares. The shade at the window was down, and stayed down till broad daylight.

Gladys said she should have been able to stand it for six weeks. They pulled down the shade every day before sunset. She saw the faces only that one time, and she never could remember a single one of those horrible dreams. But she always knew that the faces were outside that shade trying to look in, and she couldn't stand it. One day she just left. She went to the depot and bought a ticket with almost all of her money and left on the next train, with a few things wrapped in a bundle. She did not take any of the things that Amy's folks had given her, and afterward she wrote to them and tried to explain but she never mailed the letters.

What happened to Gladys after that doesn't belong to this account. I do not remember when or why she left the Postal's Midland Hotel branch office, and I have heard nothing of her since then. Her inexplicable experience in Mayfield, Kentucky, was only a chapter in the short but adventurous autobiography that she told me in vivid bits while we curled and combed our hair in the sophisticated luxury of the Midland's public dressing room on the mezzanine. I do not remember that we discussed it all; I would certainly have forgotten it but for subsequent events.

In 1908 I was manager of the Western Union's office in Mount Vernon, Indiana. I was also telegraph operator, clerk cashier, janitress, and stern though frequently baffled chief of the staff, one messenger boy aged 13. Mine was a position of dignity, leisure, and affluence; I worked only ten hours a day, only six days a week, and my salary was $50 a month. I lived well, dressed fashionably, and every payday gaily added $25 to my savings bank account.

The memory lingers with me still of those huge, delicious 5-cent sandwiches, buttered buns enfolding a major portion of a sizzling fried fish fresh-caught from the Ohio.

One day a briskly important young man breezed (as he would have said) into the office, dashed off (as he would have said) exactly ten words on a telegraph blank, and swirled it around on the counter to me. It was the routine message from husband to wife, announcing his arrival and ending, "Meet me," as such messages always did. I was surprised to hear myself exclaiming the address aloud, "Mayfield, Kentucky!"

"Oh, you know Mayfield?" the customer said. In some confusion, I said that I didn't. He guessed, then, that I'd been reading about the excitement there, in the newspapers. I hadn't; then as now I was unperturbed in placid ignorance of the newspapers.

Unquestionably my first surmise had been correct; this customer was what I would have called "a traveling man"; in 1908 only a hayseed still said "drummer." He pushed his hat back, lounged jauntily against the counter, and told me all about the excitement in Mayfield.

There had been an old house there, he said, in the edge of the town on the bank of the river. It was a ramshackle old place, nobody had lived in it for years; there were stories that it was haunted, but nobody pays any attention to such notions any more, do they kiddo? Well, here last week the railroad was putting in a new sidetrack, and they had to widen the flats along the river, where the railroad yards are, so they wrecked the old place and brought in steam-shovels and dug into the bank underneath where it was, and what do you suppose they dug up? Bones, girlie, human bones. It's in all the newspapers. They got reporters there, taking pictures, from St. Louis and Chicago and everywhere. It's a big sensation, a BIG one.

Yes siree sir, those steam-shovels have brought to light any amount of skeletons. Skeletons of old men and women and middle-aged, and young ones, children, they say even babies. They haven't sorted them all out yet, but there's dozens of skulls and skeletons, some say hundreds. Buried all these years under that old house. And it turns out, the papers say, that that old place was an inn, once, in the early days before Mayfield was built, when the early settlers were coming west. They say there was a good many such places, along the trails, that took in travelers and their families for the night and then murdered them in their beds and buried their bodies, for whatever goods they had with them. They had horses or oxen and wagons, and their supplies, of course, and guns and clothes, and these inn-keepers murdered them in cold blood, for things like that. Whole families. And now those steam-shovels are digging up their bones. Though they've stopped them now; there's men there digging now with picks and shovels, it seems more respectful to the dead. But nobody even knows their names today. There's probably no way to trace them. Nobody'll ever know who they were. Nothing but bones. Lying there all these years under that old house. It gives you something to think about, don't it?

I said yes, it did.

He said that it was a big excitement in Mayfield, the biggest sensation maybe that Mayfield ever had yet, and I certainly ought to read the papers, a big sensation like that even in St. Louis and Chicago and probably New York by this time.

I said I certainly ought to read about it; I said, "This will be twenty-five cents," and he paid for the telegram and left. I didn't remember his name and I did not read the papers. I thought of Gladys, but I had not thought of her for years and didn't know where she was.

As everyone knows, a mention of the supernatural in any group of persons will produce strange anecdotes. Someone or several in the group will relate an absolutely trustworthy friend's inexplicable experience. The narrator does not believe in ghosts, of course; no one present does; but can you explain this actual occurrence? The traveling man's sequel to Gladys' tale was a coincidence that served me well in such anecdotal groups, for many years. I thought the story ended, but it was not.

In 1928 I completed the typical American circle by returning from Baghdad via Tirana, to the farm from which I had set out. This farm is near Mansfield, Missouri, The Gem City of the Ozarks, pop. 811. I like it; I like Mansfield and Mansfield people and the Ozarks, their sea-level blue skyline, their clear limestone streams, their early blossoming springtimes, their incredible massed expanses of summer's wild flowers, their winters brown with oak leaves, their fox chases and frolics and speeding motor cars filled with singers playing guitars.

Mr. N. J. Craig was President of the Farmers and Merchants Bank in Mansfield. The Craigs and my family were old friends, and often I listened entranced to an eveningful of Mr. Craig's stories and modestly tried to repay him with some of my own. So one day when Mr. Craig telephoned to ask if he might bring an acquaintance out to tea, I was pleased, and I thought nothing of it when, over the teacups, he asked me to tell the anecdote about the haunted house in Mayfield, Kentucky.

I told it unusually well, I thought, for no one had ever listened more attentively or appreciatively than Mr. Craig's acquaintance. He was a quiet young man, intelligent, somewhat reserved but observant and quick-witted; the perfect listener who doesn't miss or fumble the most subtle nuance. I finished the tale; there was a brief pause. Then he thanked me.

"It is an extraordinary story," he said. "I think I have never heard a stranger one, and I am greatly obliged to you for telling it to me. I cannot explain it at all. Because, you see, I was born and brought up in Mayfield, Kentucky; I have lived there all my life and live there now. And there is no river in or near Mayfield, Kentucky."

HE WALKED BY DAY

Julius Long

Friedenburg, Ohio, sleeps between the muddy waters of the Miami River and the trusty track of a little-used spur of the Big Four. It suddenly became important to us because of its strategic position. It bisected a road which we were to surface with tar. The materials were to come by way of the spur and to be unloaded at the tiny yard.

We began work on a Monday morning. I was watching the tar distributor while it pumped tar from the car, when I felt a tap upon my back. I turned about, and when I beheld the individual who had tapped me, I actually jumped.

I have never, before or since, encountered such a singular figure. He was at least seven feet tall, and he seemed even taller than that because of the uncommon slenderness of his frame. He looked as if he had never been warmed by the rays of the sun, but confined all his life in a dank and dismal cellar. I concluded that he had been the prey of some insidious, etiolating disease. Certainly, I thought, nothing else could account for his ashen complexion. It seems that not blood, but shadows passed through his veins.

"Do you want to see me?" I asked.

"Are you the road feller?"

"Yes."

"I want a job. My mother's sick. I have her to keep. Won't you please give me a job?"

We really didn't need another man, but I was interested in this pallid giant with his staring, gray eyes. I called to Juggy, my foreman.

"Do you think we can find a place for this fellow?" I asked.

Juggy stared incredulously. "He looks like he'd break in two."

"I'm stronger'n anyone," said the youth.

He looked about, and his eyes fell on the Mack, which had just been loaded with six tons of gravel. He walked over to it, reached down and seized the hub of a front wheel. To our utter amazement, the wheel was slowly lifted from the ground. When it was raised to a height of eight or nine inches, the youth looked inquiringly in our direction. We must have appeared sufficiently awed, for he dropped the wheel with an abruptness that evoked a yell from the driver, who thought his tire would blow out.

"We can certainly use this fellow," I said, and Juggy agreed.

"What's your name, Shadow?" he demanded.

"Karl Rand," said the boy but "Shadow" stuck to him, as far as the crew was concerned.

We put him to work at once, and he slaved all morning, accomplishing tasks that we ordinarily assigned two or three men to do.

We were on the road at lunchtime, some miles from Friedenburg. I recalled that Shadow had not brought his lunch.

"You can take mine," I said. "I'll drive in to the village and eat."

"I never eat none," was Shadow's astonishing remark.

"You never eat!" The crew had heard his assertion, and there was an amused crowd about him at once. I fancied that he was pleased to have an audience.

"No, I never eat," he repeated. "You see"—he lowered his voice—"you see, I'm a ghost!"

We exchanged glances. So Shadow was psychopathic. We shrugged our shoulders.

"Whose ghost are you?" gibed Juggy. "Napoleon's?"

"Oh, no. I'm my own ghost. You see, I'm dead."

"Ah!" This was all Juggy could say. For once, the arch-kidder was nonplussed.

"That's why I'm so strong," added Shadow.

"How long have you been dead?" I asked.

"Six years. I was fifteen years old then."

"Tell us how it happened. Did you die a natural death, or were you killed trying to lift a fast freight off the track?" This question was asked by Juggy, who was slowly recovering.

"It was in the cave," answered Shadow solemnly. "I slipped and fell over a bank. I cracked my head on the floor. I've been a ghost ever since."

"Then why do you walk by day instead of by night?"

"I got to keep my mother."

Shadow looked so sincere, so pathetic when he made this answer, that we left off teasing him. I tried to make him eat my lunch, but he would have none of it. I expected to see him collapse that afternoon, but he worked steadily and showed no sign of tiring. We didn't know what to make of him. I confess that I was a little afraid in his presence. After all, a madman with almost superhuman strength is a dangerous character. But Shadow seemed perfectly harmless and docile.

When we had returned to our boarding-house that night, we plied our landlord with questions about Karl Rand. He drew himself up authoritatively, and lectured for some minutes upon Shadow's idiosyncrasies.

"The boy first started telling that story about six years ago," he said. "He never was right in his head, and nobody paid much attention to him at first. He said he'd fallen and busted his head in a cave, but everybody knows they ain't no caves hereabouts. I don't know what put that idea in his head. But Karl's stuck to it ever since, and I 'spect they's lots of folks round Friedenburg that's growed to believe him—more'n admits they do."

That evening, I patronized the village barber shop, and was careful to introduce Karl's name into the conversation. "All I can say is," said the barber solemnly, "that his hair ain't growed any in the last six years, and they was nary a whisker on his chin. No, sir, nary a whisker on his chin."

This did not strike me as so tremendously odd, for I had previously heard of cases of such arrested growth. However, I went to sleep that night thinking about Shadow.

The next morning, the strange youth appeared on time and rode with the crew to the job.

"Did you eat well?" Juggy asked him.

Shadow shook his head. "I never eat none."

The crew half believed him.

Early in the morning, Steve Bradshaw, the nozzle man on the tar distributer, burned his hand badly. I hurried him in to see the village doctor. When he had dressed Steve's hand, I took advantage of my opportunity and made inquiries about Shadow.

"Karl's got me stumped," said the country practitioner. "I confess I can't understand it. Of course, he won't let me get close enough to him to look at him, but it don't take an examination to tell there's something abnormal about him."

"I wonder what could have given him the idea that he's his own ghost," I said.

"I'm not sure, but I think what put it in his head was the things people used to say to him when he was a kid. He always looked like a ghost, and everybody kidded him about it. I kind of think that's what gave him the notion."

"Has he changed at all in the last six years?"

"Not a bit. He was as tall six years ago as he is today. I think that his abnormal growth might have had something to do with the stunting of his mind. But I don't know for sure."

I had to take Steve's place on the tar distributor during the next four days, and I watched Shadow pretty closely. He never ate any lunch, but he would sit with us while we devoured ours. Juggy could not resist the temptation to joke at his expense.

"There was a ghost back in my home town," Juggy once told him. "Mary Jenkens was an awful pretty woman when she was living, and when she was a girl, every fellow in town wanted to marry her. Jim Jenkens finally led her down the aisle, and we was all jealous—especially Joe Garver. He was broke up awful. Mary hadn't no more'n come back from the Falls when Joe was trying to make up to her. She wouldn't have nothing to do with him. Joe was hurt bad.

"A year after she was married, Mary took sick and died. Jim Jenkens was awful put out about it. He didn't act right from then on. He got to imagining things. He got suspicious of Joe.

"'What you got to worry about?' people would ask him. 'Mary's dead. There can't no harm come to her now.'

"But Jim didn't feel that way. Joe heard about it, and he got to teasing Jim.

"'I was out with Mary's ghost last night,' he would say. And Jim got to believing him. One night, he lays low for Joe and shoots him with both barrels. 'He was goin' to meet my wife!' Jim told the judge."

"Did they give him the chair?" I asked.

"No, they gave him life in the state hospital."

Shadow remained impervious to Juggy's yarns, which were told for his special benefit. During this time, I noticed something decidedly strange about the boy, but I kept my own counsel. After all, a contractor can not keep the respect of his men if he appears too credulous.

One day Juggy voiced my suspicions for me. "You know," he said, "I never saw that kid sweat. It's uncanny. It's ninety in the shade today, and Shadow ain't got a drop of perspiration on his face. Look at his shirt. Dry as if he'd just put it on."

Everyone in the crew noticed this. I think we all became uneasy in Shadow's presence.

One morning he didn't show up for work. We waited a few minutes and left without him. When the trucks came in with their second load of gravel, the drivers told us that Shadow's mother had died during the night. This news cast a gloom over the crew. We all sympathized with the youth.

"I wish I hadn't kidded him," said Juggy.

We all put in an appearance that evening at Shadow's little cottage, and I think he was tremendously gratified. "I won't be working no more," he told me. "There ain't no need for me now."

I couldn't afford to lay off the crew for the funeral, but I did go myself. I even accompanied Shadow to the cemetery.

We watched while the grave was being filled. There were many others there, for one of the chief delights in a rural community is to see how the mourners "take on" at a funeral. Moreover, their interest in Karl Rand was deeper. He had said he was going back to his cave, that he would never again walk by day. The villagers, as well as myself, wanted to see what would happen.

When the grave was filled, Shadow turned to me, eyed me pathetically a moment, then walked from the grave. Silently, we watched him set out across the field. Two mischievous boys disobeyed the entreaties of their parents, and set out after him.

They returned to the village an hour later with a strange and incredible story. They had seen Karl disappear into the ground. The earth had literally swallowed him up. The youngsters were terribly frightened. It was thought that Karl had done something to scare them, and their imaginations had got the better of them.

But the next day they were asked to lead a group of the more curious to the spot where Karl had vanished. He had not returned, and they were worried.

In a ravine two miles from the village, the party discovered a small but penetrable entrance to a cave. Its existence had never been dreamed of by the farmer who owned the land. (He has since then opened it up for tourists, and it is known as Ghost Cave.)

Someone in the party had thoughtfully brought an electric searchlight, and the party squeezed its way into the cave. Exploration revealed a labyrinth of caverns of exquisite beauty. But the explorers were oblivious to the esthetics of the cave; they thought only of Karl and his weird story.

After circuitous ramblings, they came to a sudden drop in the floor. At the base of this precipice they beheld a skeleton.

The coroner and the sheriff were duly summoned. The sheriff invited me to accompany him.

I regret that I cannot describe the gruesome, awesome feeling that came over me as I made my way through those caverns. Within their chambers the human voice is given a peculiar sepulchral sound. But perhaps it was the knowledge of Karl's bizarre story, his unaccountable disappearance that inspired me with such awe, such thoughts.

The skeleton gave me a shock, for it was a skeleton of a man seven feet tall! There was no mistake about this; the coroner was positive.

The skull had been fractured, apparently by a fall over the bank. It was I who discovered the hat near by. It was rotted with decay, but in the leather band were plainly discernible the crudely penned initials, "K. R."

I felt suddenly weak. The sheriff noticed my nervousness. "What's the matter; have you seen a ghost?"

I laughed nervously and affected nonchalance. With the best off-hand manner I could command, I told him of Karl Rand. He was not impressed.

"You don't—?" He did not wish to insult my intelligence by finishing his question.

At this moment, the coroner looked up and commented: "This skeleton has been here about six years, I'd say."

I was not courageous enough to acknowledge my suspicions, but the villagers were outspoken. The skeleton, they declared, was that of Karl Rand. The coroner and the sheriff were incredulous, but, politicians both, they displayed some sympathy with this view.

My friend, the sheriff, discussed the matter privately with me some days later. His theory was that Karl had discovered the cave, wandered inside and come upon the corpse of some unfortunate who had preceded him. He had been so excited by his discovery that his hat had fallen down beside the body. Later, aided by the remarks of the villagers about his ghostliness, he had fashioned his own legend.

This, of course, may be true. But the people of Friedenburg are not convinced by this explanation, and neither am I. For the identity of the skeleton has never been determined, and Karl Rand has never since been seen to walk by day.

THE WENDIGO

Alvin Schwartz

A wealthy man wanted to go hunting in a part of northern Canada where few people had ever hunted. He traveled to a trading post and tried to find a guide to take him. But no one would do it. It was too dangerous, they said.

Finally, he found an Indian who needed money badly, and he agreed to take him. The Indian's name was DéFago.

They made camp in the snow near a large frozen lake. For three days they hunted, but they had nothing to show for it. The third night a windstorm came up. They lay in their tent listening to the wind howling and the trees whipping back and forth.

To see the storm better, the hunter opened the tent flap. What he saw startled him. There wasn't a breath of air stirring, and the trees were standing perfectly still. Yet he could hear the wind howling. And the more he listened, the more it sounded as if it were calling DéFago's name.

"Da-faaaaaaaaay-go!" it called. "Da-faaaa-aaaaay-go!"

"I must be losing my mind," the hunter thought.

But DéFago had gotten out of his sleeping bag. He was huddled in a corner of the tent, his head buried in his arms.

"What's this all about?" the hunter asked.

"It's nothing," DéFago said.

But the wind continued to call to him. And DéFago became more tense and more restless.

"Da-Faaaaaaaaay-go!" it called. "Da-faaaaa-aaaay-go!"

Suddenly, he jumped to his feet, and he began to run from the tent. But the hunter grabbed him and wrestled him to the ground.

"You can't leave me out here," the hunter shouted. Then the wind called again, and DéFago broke loose and ran into the darkness. The hunter could hear him screaming as he went. Again and again he cried, "Oh, my fiery feet, my burning feet of fire . . ." Then his voice faded away, and the wind died down.

At daybreak, the hunter followed DéFago's tracks in the snow. They went through the woods, down toward the lake, then out onto the ice.

But soon he noticed something strange. The steps DéFago had taken got longer and longer. They were so long no human being could have taken them. It was as if something had helped him to hurry away.

The hunter followed the tracks out to the middle of the lake, but there they disappeared. At first, he thought that DéFago had fallen through the ice, but there wasn't any hole. Then he thought that something had pulled him off the ice into the sky. But that made no sense.

As he stood wondering what had happened, the wind picked up again. Soon it was howling as it had the night before. Then he heard DéFago's voice. It was coming from up above, and again he heard DéFago screaming, ". . . My fiery feet, my burning feet . . ." But there was nothing to be seen.

Now the hunter wanted to leave that place as fast as he could. He went back to camp and packed. Then he left some food for DéFago, and he started out. Weeks later he reached civilization.

The following year he went back to hunt in that area again. He went to the same trading post to look for a guide. The people there could not explain what had happened to DéFago that night. But they had not seen him since then.

"Maybe it was the Wendigo," one of them said, and he laughed. "It's supposed to come with the wind. It drags you along at great speed until your feet are burned away, and more of you than that. Then it carries you into the sky, and it drops you. It's just a crazy story, but that's what some of the Indians say."

A few days later the hunter was at the trading post again. An Indian came in and sat by the fire. He had a blanket wrapped around him, and he wore his hat so that you couldn't see his face. The hunter thought there was something familiar about him.

He walked over and he asked, "Are you DéFago?"

The Indian didn't answer.

"Do you know anything about him?"

No answer.

He began to wonder if something was wrong, if the man needed help. But he couldn't see his face.

"Are you all right?" he asked.

No answer.

To get a look at him, he lifted the Indian's hat. Then he screamed. There was nothing under the hat but a pile of ashes.

THE SEVERED HAND

Janice M. Del Negro

Fair Mary was merry. Fair Mary was kind. She had more brothers than you can count on one hand, for she had seven. Her brothers had raised her from a babe, for their parents had died when she was very young. A fine job they'd done of it, too, for there were many young men who wanted to marry Mary. The blacksmith's son, the minister's nephew, the butcher's boy— they came courting every Sunday and sat in the parlor, trying their country best to charm her. But Mary was not interested in any of these young men. She had known them all her life, and, if truth be told, they bored her to distraction. She longed to meet a man unlike any other she had met before, someone mysterious and exciting. And you know what they say. Be careful what you wish for.

One day there came to town a man unlike any other Mary had ever met. He was tall and straight, with bright green eyes and shocking red hair. His clothes were elegant, and his manner even more so. His name was Mr. Fox, and soon, very soon, he began courting Mary. He would come by on Sunday and sit in the parlor and tell her stories of his travels, of all the exotic places he had been, and the strange and unusual sights he had seen. It wasn't long before the other young men stopped coming, for it was clear Mary had made her choice. The engagement was soon announced, to the chagrin of the country suitors, and to the delight of the headstrong Mary.

Now, Mr. Fox spoke to Mary of his manor house on the other side of the woods, filled with the curious and beautiful things collected on his travels. "You must come and see the house, my Mary," he would say. "For soon you will be mistress there." But although they spoke often of such a visit, somehow it was never arranged.

One Saturday Mary was walking through the woods, and, what with thinking of this and thinking of that, she wandered deeper into the woods than she ever had ventured before. The light was fading, but she was not frightened, not then. She knew that if she stayed on the path, it would curve back to meet the road, and she would easily find her way home, daylight or no, so she continued on. Soon she came to a clearing, and on the edge of the clearing was a great house. She knew it was the home of Mr. Fox, for he had described it to her. "Well, then, this is good fortune," she thought. "I will knock on the door, and Mr. Fox will give me something cool to drink, and perhaps a ride back to town." Across the fragrant meadow she went, and up the great front steps to the great front door. Raising her hand to knock, Mary looked up. Carved above the great front door were the words "Be bold. Be bold."

She did not know what it meant. "A family motto," thought Mary. "I must gain its meaning from my Mr. Fox." Being bold enough, she knocked on the door. The sound of her knocking echoed inside the house, echoed on and back, but no one came. "Now this is strange," Mary thought, "for in a house this large, there should be many servants." She knocked again, and again there was no answer, and thinking only to herself, "Oh, Mr. Fox, he would not mind," Mary turned the golden doorknob until the door opened smoothly beneath her hand.

She stepped into a great hall that fairly took her breath. Beneath her feet was a marble floor polished to mirror brightness. Above her head was a crystal chandelier that glittered in the afternoon sun, and curving up to the second floor was a long stairway, wide and graceful. Mary looked at the elegant stairway and imagined herself sweeping down the stairs, her stairs, on the arm of Mr. Fox, her Mr. Fox, making a grand entrance into the grand hall. Thinking only to herself, "Oh, Mr. Fox, he would not mind," Mary ran lightly up the stairs, intending only to sweep down them again. But at the top of the stairs there was another door and carved above the door were the words "Be bold. Be bold. But not too bold." She did not know what they meant, but nevertheless, she was bold enough.

She opened the second door and stepped into the most richly appointed bedroom she had ever seen. The walls hung with tapestries embroidered in gold, the bed was covered with velvet, the floor with carpets in colors that glowed like fire. And across the room, there was yet another door, a third door, a closet door.

Now closets in those days were not like closets today, but more like small rooms. A person could step inside them, the clothes hanging about the walls. Mary thought of the elegant clothes Mr. Fox always wore, never the same twice since she had known him, and wondered if there was room in that closet for her clothes. Thinking only to herself, "Oh, Mr. Fox, he would not mind," she crossed the room. Carved above the closet door were the words "Be bold. Be bold. But not too bold. Lest your heart's blood run cold." Mary did not know what the words meant, but she did not let that stop her. Mary opened the door and stepped inside.

It took a few moments for her eyes to adjust to darkness. When they had, she saw before her three great cauldrons, huge iron pots. She stepped up to the first and saw that it was full of human hair. Red, gold, black, and brown gleamed in the shadowy light. Her heart began to beat a little faster. Mary stepped to the second cauldron and saw that it was filled with human bones. She knew they were human bones; she could tell by the skulls gleaming there in the half-light, and her heart beat faster still. Mary stepped to the third cauldron and saw that it was full of some dark liquid. She dipped her fingertips into the liquid, smelled it, and knew that it was blood.

Heart in her throat, Mary backed up against the closet wall. She thought she would be sick. Hands over her mouth to keep from screaming, she ran from the closet, slamming the door behind her.

Across the bedroom she ran, slamming that door behind her, too. She started down the great curving stair. And that was when she saw him. Through the front window she saw him, Mr. Fox, coming across the meadow dragging a young woman behind him. Mary was trapped there on the stairs. She could not go up. She could not go out. She ran down the long curved stairway and hid in the shadows beneath it.

The great front door flew open, and Mr. Fox entered, dragging the young woman across the gleaming marble floor. He pulled her up the stairs. In a last desperate effort to save herself, the young woman reached out and grabbed hold of the banister and Mr. Fox, without missing a beat, drew his sword and cut off her hand. The hand flew through the air and landed in Mary's lap, where she crouched hidden beneath the stair. She knew her life was forfeit if he discovered her. Mary heard the bedroom door open and close, then the closet door, then silence. She wrapped the severed hand in her apron and ran from Mr. Fox's lair. She ran across the meadow. She ran through the woods. She did not stop running until she reached the safety of her brothers' house.

The next day was Sunday, and as was his habit, Mr. Fox came to visit Mary. They sat in the parlor, Mary's back to the heavy drapes that shut out the wind and weather, and although Mr. Fox's stories were as witty as ever, she was strangely silent.

Finally, Mr. Fox said to her, "Mary, my dear, what is it? You do not seem yourself today."

And Mary replied, "Oh, Mr. Fox, last night I had a dream."

"A dream?" said Mr. Fox. "I am very good at interpreting dreams. You tell me what you dreamt, and I will tell you what it meant."

And so Mary began.

"I dreamed I was walking through the woods, and I came to a great clearing. On the edge of the clearing was a great house, and carved above the great front door were the words 'Be bold. Be bold.'"

"But it was not so," said Mr. Fox.

"In my dream, sir, in my dream it was so. In my dream I opened the great front door and went into a great hall. Up a curving stair there was a second door and carved above it were the words 'Be bold. Be bold. But not too bold.'"

"But it was not so," said Mr. Fox. "And it is not so."

"In my dream, sir, it was so, in my dream. In my dream I opened the second door, and across a rich bedroom was yet a third door, and carved above it the words 'Be bold. Be bold. But not too bold. Lest your heart's blood run cold.' I opened the third door and within found three cauldrons, one full of human hair, one full of human bones, and one full of human blood. I ran from that room, sir, down the stair. And then I saw you, Mr. Fox, I saw you, coming across the meadow, dragging a young woman by the hair. You pulled her up the stair, and when she reached out to save herself, you drew your sword and cut off her hand."

Mr. Fox had gone very pale. "But it was not so!" he cried. "And it is not so. And God forbid that it should be so."

"Ah, but it was so. And it is so. And here is the hand to prove it so." And between them on the table she laid that severed hand.

Mr. Fox stood so quickly his chair fell over behind him. His green green eyes glittered in his pale pale face, and his hand was on his sword. In a deadly whisper he said, "Ah, it was so. And it is so, but you are the only one who knows, and you will never tell."

Mary stood and threw open the drapes behind her. Her seven brothers fell on Mr. Fox, and, dragging him to the back of the house, they did to him there what he had done to so many others.

KNOCK, KNOCK, WHO'S THERE?

J. J. Reneaux

This is a blending of two family stories passed down through my family and told for true. It's a good example of how stories evolve from real events, and survive time and distance to become folktales. The story is based on a fact. Buried coffins did indeed float up during flooding—hence the practice of burying the dead above the ground in vaults and "ovens" (wall vaults). According to family legend, one of my ancestors was too cheap to properly bury his wife and, when the land flooded, she floated up and knocked against the house, so terrifying her miserly old husband that he went mad by morning. The rest of the story as I have presented it is based on the further legend of my poor Tante Claire. As the story goes, when she was sixteen, she knocked on her father's door one night, complaining of being sick, but he thought she was just putting on and refused to get her any medical help. By the time he realized just how sick his daughter really was, it was too late. She died on the kitchen table while the unprepared country doctor tried to perform an emergency appendectomy with a butcher knife.

Around La Ville, New Orleans, the land is so low and wet that the dead have to be buried above ground in a vault. Folks don't bury their dead in a grave in the ground. If the river were to overflow the *levée,* or a hurricane to flood the land, your loved one might just float back up from the grave and pay you a return visit!

Down the river a little ways from La Ville, there once lived an old man with his only child, a *jolie fille* called Thérèse. Her *maman* had died and Thérèse was left in the care of her papa, a greedy, miserly man who worked his girl like a mule and dressed her in rags. Though she was of a marrying age, he would not allow any young man to court her. She saw no one except her mean ol' papa.

All he ever cared for were the gold coins that he kept hidden under a loose board in the floor beneath his bed. Every night he'd lock the door, and by the light of a flickering candle, he'd count his golden coins. He loved the way they clinked and glowed and weighed so heavy in his hands. But poor Thérèse, she was so lonesome. Every night she'd come knocking on his door, knock, knock. Her papa would yell out, "Who's there?"

"Papa, *c'est moi,*" she'd say. "It's me, Thérèse. Papa, let me in, talk with me. I am so lonely!"

But her papa would only holler back at her, "Girl, get on outta here and get back to work. You only wanta get your hands on my gold, and thatta be over my dead body!"

And so it went until one night, knock, knock. "Who's there?" "Papa, it's me, Thérèse. Me, I'm sick-sick," she moans. "Papa, let me in!"

But he just yells back, "You lazy good-for-nothin'! Get outta here. You're not sick. You just wanta get your hands on my money, and thatta be over my dead body!"

Again and again Thérèse returned to her father's door, knock, knock.

"Who's there?"

"Papa, *c'est moi.* Papa, let me in. I'm bad sick. I need the healer. Please, Papa, send for the *traiteur!*"

Knock, knock.

"Who's there?"

"Papa, please help me. The pain is worse. Oh, Papa, open the door!"

But her papa's heart was as cold as his golden coins. At last the girl's cries faded to silence, and she knocked no more. The old man was full of curiosity, and so he opened the door. There, lying lifeless on the porch floor, was *jolie* Thérèse.

The old man was too stingy to buy a vault for his daughter. Instead, he laid Thérèse in a crude wooden coffin and buried her in a shallow, swampy grave down by the cypress tree. The neighbors all shook their heads. They warned there would be trouble. How could poor Thérèse rest in peace in such a grave?

Three weeks went by and a storm began to coil up out over the gulf. The winds churned and rain fell like needles as the hurricane passed over the land. Night found the old man sitting in his room counting his gold coins by flickering candlelight.

Outside, the wind howled and blew sheets of rain against the house. The old man did not know that the river had already spilled over the *levée* and sent its dark water across the land. He sat in his rocking chair, his lap full of gold, rocking and counting, "*Un, deux, trois . . .*"

Something thumped against his porch with a hollow wooden clatter. Knock, knock, knock sounded at his door.

"Who's there?" he hollers.

Only a great sigh like the wind answered. "Just a loose shutter bangin'," he thinks, and went on counting his shining gold. "*Un, deux, trois . . .*"

Knock, knock, knock pounded at his door, stronger this time.

"Who's there?"

Only a whining wind answered him. "Just that good-for-nothin' hound dog tryin' to get in," he thinks. Again he returned to his golden coins. "*Un, deux, trois . . .*"

Knock, knock, knock! Three great booming knocks hammered at his door.

"Who's there?"

Only a low, sad moaning. A cold shiver ran down the old man's back. "Storm's gotcha all jumpy," he says to himself. "It's just the wind blowin' that ol' live oak tree, scrapin' its branches against the house."

But the moaning rose and rose above the wailing wind until it became a horrifying scream.

"Papa, *c'est moi*, Thérèse! Let me in! It's me, Thérèse!" Knock, knock, knock! "Papa, let me in!" Knock, knock, knock! "Papa, let me innnnnn!"

As the eye of the storm passed over the house, a bloodcurdling shriek pierced the deadly calm.

Three days passed and the waters receded. Neighbors came by to look in on the old man. They rode onto his land, and as they passed by the cypress tree they saw that the flood had washed all the dirt away from Thérèse's grave and it was empty.

They knocked at the back door but no voice answered. Fearing some harm had befallen the old man, they went inside. They found him sitting like stone in his rocking chair, cold as marble, his hair gone snow white. A silent scream was frozen on his face, and his eyes bulged in glassy terror.

Across the room, the door hung limp from one hinge, as though some monstrous fist had pounded it down. Before it lay a battered, splintered coffin and, inside, the gruesome corpse of Thérèse. Her withered hands clutched her papa's golden coins, and a ghastly smile lay fixed upon her decaying lips.

With the money, the neighbors bought Thérèse a whitewashed vault and gave her a proper aboveground burial. There was not enough money to buy the old man a vault, so they buried him in a pine coffin down by the cypress tree. Since that time, whenever the river threatens to flood the land, the old man's troubled spirit rises to warn all that danger is at hand. Folks know he's paid them a visit when they hear someone knock, knock, knocking at their door but nobody is ever there!

MA YARWOOD'S
WEDDING RING

Rita Cox

There is an old house in the village. Empty, weather-beaten and covered with vines, it stands on a large plot of land. The villagers say that that house is haunted, and they talk in whispers about what happened there, a long, long time ago.

The house used to be the home of Ma and Pa Yarwood. They had known each other since they were twelve years old, had married young, and were devoted to each other for over fifty-six years.

Pa Yarwood made a good living by driving rich people in his grand old Model T Ford, which he had worked and saved to acquire. He had looked after that vehicle with love and care. On Sundays, Ma and Pa Yarwood dressed in their best and went driving in style to the nearby town. The villagers were very proud of them.

The neighbours had great love and respect for the Yarwoods, and when Pa died, they looked after the grieving widow as if she was their grandmother, checking on her every day to ensure that she was all right.

Every day Ma Yarwood came to the village store. Her dark clothing, bowed head and shuffling steps did not obscure the strength, quiet dignity and determination that her neighbours had always recognized.

One day, a stranger whose name was Cyrus came to the village. He was talking with some of the village youths outside the store when Ma Yarwood came along. He observed the respect and deference with which young and old alike greeted this old lady. "Mornin', Ma," they called, and she answered, "Mornin', my children." He noticed something else, too. He saw that Ma wore a broad gold wedding ring on her finger.

"She must be rich," he said to himself. Then he asked the young men, "Who is that old lady?"

"Oh, that's Ma Yarwood. She lives in the big house up the hill. We have known her all our lives. She and her husband were always kind and generous to all of us in the village, but he died two years ago. They say that he left her quite well off."

"Does she live alone now?" Cyrus asked.

"Yes, she does, but the people in the village look after her and make sure she is safe and well."

Cyrus thought to himself, "I hope what they say is true. If she does live alone, it would be easy to break into that house. If she's wealthy, as they say, then this should be a good night for me."

That night Cyrus took a cab to the corner of the road that led to the Yarwood house. There were no street lights in the village; the only light on that dark night came from the flashlight that Cyrus carried. He came to the old house, climbed the steps and pushed the front door. It was open. Cyrus crept in. He went from room to room, searching through drawers, cupboards, shelves. He ransacked the furniture, looked behind the pictures on the wall, and everywhere he could think of, but found nothing of value to him. Angry and disappointed, he made his way quietly along a narrow corridor that led to the bedroom where Ma lay asleep. Slowly, he pushed the door. It creaked loudly, and Ma awoke.

Alarmed, she shouted out, "Who are you! What do you want!"

"Be quiet and stay where you are," said Cyrus.

But Ma got out of bed with surprising agility and rushed to the intruder, arms upraised, fists clenched.

Cyrus grabbed the old lady by the shoulders. "Stop screaming! Shut your mouth, or I'll kill you!"

Ma struggled and fought. Her strength and resistance surprised Cyrus, and he panicked. He placed his hands on Ma's throat. He squeezed and squeezed, until Ma fell to the floor, eyes staring. Cyrus stepped over Ma Yarwood's body. He turned up the mattress, he tossed things out of the dresser drawers, tore the wardrobe apart; he looked everywhere, but he found nothing. This journey was all in vain.

He turned to leave. As he stepped over the old woman's body, the light from his flashlight caught the glint of the ring. He bent down and tore the ring from her finger, and rushed from the house.

On the main road he hailed a lone cab going to town. He climbed into the back seat. Cyrus was lost in his own angry thoughts when the cab driver spoke.

"What on earth is an old woman doing on the road at this hour of the night?" he asked.

From the light of the cab's headlights, Cyrus could see a bent figure walking slowly on the side of the road ahead.

When he came alongside, the driver stopped the car and called out, "Granny, where are you going at this hour?"

The old lady pointed ahead.

"Get in, Granny. I'll take you there." Turning to Cyrus, he said, "I hope you don't mind. We villagers look after each other."

Cyrus didn't answer. The old woman opened the back door and got in beside him. The driver started the car again and, as he drove, the old woman shifted closer and closer to the passenger. He crouched farther and farther in the corner. She moved closer and closer to him. Then the old woman reached out, took hold of Cyrus's right hand and pulled off the ring he had just stolen.

Terrified, Cyrus looked into her face. He took one look into those staring eyes, opened the car door and jumped out—right into the path of a vehicle coming the other way.

The cab driver stepped on his brakes, stopped the car and got out. The old woman had vanished. The passenger lay dead on the road, and the vehicle that hit him was nowhere to be seen. The police arrived. The bewildered cab driver explained the accident as best he could. "This young man jumped out of my car, into the path of an old car the like of which I haven't seen in years. It was a Model T Ford. It appeared as if from nowhere. It vanished as mysteriously as it appeared. There was an old woman in my backseat as well, and she too disappeared. These were strange happenings tonight. I don't understand it."

The neighbours in the village noticed that Ma Yarwood had not appeared in two days. They went to her house. There, on the floor of her bedroom, they found her, lying lifeless, eyes staring, her left hand clutched tight. They summoned the priest, the doctor and the village police. They pried open her rigid hand, and in it lay the broad, golden wedding ring that Pa Yarwood had placed on her finger over fifty years ago.

HOME

Shirley Jackson

Ethel Sloane was whistling to herself as she got out of her car and splashed across the sidewalk to the doorway of the hardware store. She was wearing a new raincoat and solid boots, and one day of living in the country had made her weather-wise. "This rain can't last," she told the hardware clerk confidently. "This time of year it never lasts."

The clerk nodded tactfully. One day in the country had been enough for Ethel Sloane to become acquainted with most of the local people; she had been into the hardware store several times—"so many odd things you never expect you're going to need in an old house"— and into the post office to leave their new address, and into the grocery to make it clear that all the Sloane grocery business was going to come their way, and into the bank and into the gas station and into the little library and even as far as the door of the barbershop (". . . and you'll be seeing my husband Jim Sloane in a day or so!"). Ethel Sloane liked having bought the old Sanderson place, and she liked walking the single street of the village, and most of all she liked knowing that people knew who she was.

"They make you feel at home right away, as though you were born not half a mile from here," she explained to her husband, Jim.

Privately she thought that the storekeepers in the village might show a little more alacrity in remembering her name; she had probably brought more business to the little stores in the village than any of them had seen for a year past. They're not outgoing people, she told herself reassuringly. It takes a while for them to get over being suspicious; we've been here in the house for only two days.

"First, I want to get the name of a good plumber," she said to the clerk in the hardware store. Ethel Sloane was a great believer in getting information directly from the local people; the plumbers listed in the phone book might be competent enough, but the local people always knew who would suit; Ethel Sloane had no intention of antagonizing the villagers by hiring an unpopular plumber. "And closet hooks," she said. "My husband, Jim, turns out to be just as good a handyman as he is a writer." Always tell them your business, she thought, then they don't have to ask.

"I suppose the best one for plumbing would be Will Watson," the clerk said. "He does most of the plumbing around. You drive down the Sanderson road in this rain?"

"Of course." Ethel Sloane was surprised. "I had all kinds of things to do in the village."

"Creek's pretty high. They say that sometimes when the creek is high—"

"The bridge held our moving truck yesterday, so I guess it will hold my car today. That bridge ought to stand for a while yet." Briefly she wondered whether she might not say "for a spell" instead of "for a while," and then decided that sooner or later it would come naturally. "Anyway, who minds rain? We've got so much to do indoors." She was pleased with "indoors."

"Well," the clerk said, "of course, no one can stop you from driving on the old Sanderson road. If you want to. You'll find people around here mostly leave it alone in the rain, though. Myself, I think it's all just gossip, but then, I don't drive out that way much, anyway."

"It's a little muddy on a day like this," Ethel Sloane said firmly, "and maybe a little scary crossing the bridge when the creek is high, but you've got to expect that kind of thing when you live in the country."

"I wasn't talking about that," the clerk said. "Closet hooks? I wonder, do we have any closet hooks."

In the grocery Ethel Sloane bought mustard and soap and pickles and flour. "All the things I forgot to get yesterday," she explained, laughing.

"You took that road on a day like this?" the grocer asked.

"It's not that bad," she said, surprised again. "I don't mind the rain."

"We don't use that road in this weather," the grocer said. "You might say there's talk about that road."

"It certainly seems to have quite a local reputation," Ethel said, and laughed. "And it's nowhere near as bad as some of the other roads I've seen around here."

"Well, I told you," the grocer said, and shut his mouth.

I've offended him, Ethel thought, I've said I think their roads are bad; these people are so jealous of their countryside.

"I guess our road is pretty muddy," she said almost apologetically. "But I'm really a very careful driver."

"You stay careful," the grocer said. "No matter what you see."

"I'm always careful." Whistling, Ethel Sloane went out and got into her car and turned in the circle in front of the abandoned railway station. Nice little town, she was thinking, and they are beginning to like us already, all so worried about my safe driving. We're the kind of people, Jim and I, who fit in a place like this; we wouldn't belong in the suburbs or some kind of a colony; we're real people. Jim will write, she thought, and I'll get one of these country women to teach me how to make bread. Watson for plumbing.

She was oddly touched when the clerk from the hardware store and then the grocer stepped to their doorways to watch her drive by. They're worrying about me, she thought. They're afraid a city gal can't manage their bad, wicked roads, and I do bet it's hell in the winter, but I can manage; I'm country now.

Her way led out of the village and then off the highway onto a dirt road that meandered between fields and an occasional farmhouse, then crossed the creek—disturbingly high after all this rain—and turned onto the steep hill that led to the Sanderson house. Ethel Sloane could see the house from the bridge across the creek, although in summer the view would be hidden by trees. It's a lovely house, she thought with a little catch of pride; I'm so lucky; up there it stands, so proud and remote, waiting for me to come home.

On one side of the hill the Sanderson land had long ago been sold off, and the hillside was dotted with small cottages and a couple of ramshackle farms; the people on that side of the hill used the other, lower, road, and Ethel Sloane was surprised and a little uneasy to perceive that the tyre marks on this road and across the bridge were all her own, coming down; no one else seemed to use this road at all. Private, anyway, she thought; maybe they've talked everyone else out of using it. She looked up to see the house as she crossed the bridge; my very own house, she thought, and then, well, our very own house, she thought, and then she saw that there were two figures standing silently in the rain by the side of the road.

Good heavens, she thought, standing there in this rain, and she stopped the car. "Can I give you a lift?" she called out, rolling down the window. Through the rain she could see that they seemed to be an old woman and a child, and the rain drove down on them. Staring, Ethel Sloane became aware that the child was sick with misery, wet and shivering and crying in the rain, and she said sharply, "Come and get in the car at once; you mustn't keep that child out in the rain another minute."

They stared at her, the old woman frowning, listening. Perhaps she is deaf, Ethel thought, and in her good raincoat and solid boots she climbed out of the car and went over to them. Not wanting for any reason in the world to touch either of them, she put her face close to the old woman's and said urgently, "Come, hurry. Get that child into the car, where it's dry. I'll take you wherever you want to go." Then, with real horror, she saw that the child was wrapped in a blanket, and under the blanket he was wearing thin pyjamas; with a shiver of fury, Ethel saw that he was barefoot and standing in the mud. "Get in that car at once," she said, and hurried to open the back door. "Get in that car at once, do you hear me?"

Silently the old woman reached her hand down to the child and, his eyes wide and staring past Ethel Sloane, the child moved towards the car, with the old woman following. Ethel looked in disgust at the small bare feet going over the mud and rocks, and she said to the old woman, "You ought to be ashamed; that child is certainly going to be sick."

She waited until they had climbed into the backseat of the car, and then slammed the door and got into her seat again. She glanced up at the mirror, but they were sitting in the corner, where she could not see them, and she turned; the child was huddled against the old woman, and the old woman looked straight ahead, her face heavy with weariness.

"Where are you going?" Ethel asked, her voice rising. "Where shall I take you? That child," she said to the old woman, "has to be gotten indoors and into dry clothes as soon as possible. Where are you going? I'll see that you get there in a hurry."

The old woman opened her mouth, and in a voice of old age beyond consolation said, "We want to go to the Sanderson place."

"To the Sanderson place?" To us? Ethel thought. To see us? This pair? Then she realized that the Sanderson place, to the old local people, probably still included the land where the cottages had been built; they probably still call the whole thing the Sanderson place, she thought, and felt oddly feudal with pride. We're the lords of the manor, she thought, and her voice was more gentle when she asked, "Were you waiting out there for very long in the rain?"

"Yes," the old woman said, her voice remote and despairing.

Their lives must be desolate, Ethel thought. Imagine being that old and that tired and standing in the rain for someone to come by. "Well, we'll soon have you home," she said, and started the car.

The wheels slipped and skidded in the mud, but found a purchase, and slowly Ethel felt the car begin to move up the hill. It was very muddy, and the rain was heavier, and the back of the car dragged as though under an intolerable weight. It's as though I had a load of iron, Ethel thought. Poor old lady, it's the weight of years.

"Is the child all right?" she asked, lifting her head; she could not turn to look at them.

"He wants to go home," the old woman said.

"I should think so. Tell him it won't be long. I'll take you right to your door." It's the least I can do, she thought, and maybe go inside with them and see that he's warm enough; those poor bare feet.

Driving up the hill was very difficult, and perhaps the road was a little worse than Ethel had believed; she found that she could not look around or even speak while she was navigating the sharp curves, with the rain driving against the windshield and the wheels slipping in the mud. Once she said, "Nearly at the top," and then had to be silent, holding the wheel tight. When the car gave a final lurch and topped the small last rise that led onto the flat driveway before the Sanderson house, Ethel said, "Made it," and laughed. "Now, which way should I go?"

They're frightened, she thought. I'm sure the child is frightened and I don't blame them; I was a little nervous myself. She said loudly, "We're at the top now, it's all right, we made it. Now where shall I take you?"

When there was still no answer, she turned; the backseat of the car was empty.

"But even if they *could* have gotten out of the car without my noticing," Ethel Sloane said for the tenth time that evening to her husband, "they couldn't have gotten out of sight. I looked and looked." She lifted her hands in an emphatic gesture. "I went all around the top of the hill in the rain looking in all directions and calling them."

"But the car seat was dry," her husband said.

"Well, you're not going to suggest that I imagined it, are you? Because I'm simply not the kind of person to dream up an old lady and a sick child. There has to be some explanation; I don't imagine things."

"Well . . ." Jim said, and hesitated.

"Are you sure you didn't see them? They didn't come to the door?"

"Listen . . ." Jim said, and hesitated again. "Look," he said.

"I have certainly never been the kind of person who goes round imagining that she sees old ladies and children. You know me better than that, Jim, you know I don't go round—"

"Well," Jim said. "Look," he said finally, "there could be something. A story I heard. I never told you because—"

"Because what?"

"Because you . . . well—" Jim said.

"Jim." Ethel Sloane set her lips. "I don't like this, Jim. What is there that you haven't told me? Is there really something you know and I don't?"

"It's just a story. I heard it when I came up to look at the house."

"Do you mean you've known something all this time and you've never told me?"

"It's just a story," Jim said helplessly. Then, looking away, he said, "Everyone knows it, but they don't say much. I mean, these things—"

"Jim," Ethel said, "tell me at once."

"It's just that there was a little Sanderson boy stolen or lost or something. They thought a crazy old woman took him. People kept talking about it, but they never knew anything for sure."

"What?" Ethel Sloane stood up and started for the door. "You mean there's a child been stolen and no one told me about it?"

"No," Jim said oddly. "I mean, it happened sixty years ago."

Ethel was still talking about it at breakfast the next morning. "And they've never been found," she told herself happily. "All the people around went searching, and they finally decided the two of them had drowned in the creek, because it was raining then just the way it is now." She glanced with satisfaction at the rain beating against the window of the breakfast room. "Oh, lovely," she said, and sighed, and stretched, and smiled. "Ghosts," she said.

"I saw two honest-to-goodness ghosts. No wonder," she said, "no wonder the child looked so awful. Awful! Kidnapped, and then drowned. No wonder."

"Listen," Jim said, "if I were you, I'd forget about it. People round here don't like to talk much about it."

"They wouldn't tell me," Ethel said, and laughed again. "Our very own ghosts, and not a soul would tell me. I just won't be satisfied until I get every word of the story."

"That's why *I* never told you," Jim said miserably.

"Don't be silly. Yesterday everyone I spoke to mentioned my driving on that road, and I bet every one of them was dying to tell me the story. I can't wait to see their faces when they hear."

"No." Jim stared at her. "You simply *can't* go round . . . *boasting* about it."

"But of course I can! Now we really belong here. I've really seen the local ghosts. And I'm going in this morning and tell everybody, and find out all I can."

"I wish you wouldn't," Jim said.

"I know you wish I wouldn't, but I'm going to. If I listened to you, I'd wait and wait for a good time to mention it and maybe even come to believe I'd dreamed it or something, so I'm going into the village right after breakfast."

"Please, Ethel," Jim said. "Please listen to me. People might not take it the way you think."

"Two ghosts of our very own." Ethel laughed again. "My very own," she said. "I just can't wait to see their faces in the village."

Before she got into the car she opened the back door and looked again at the seat, dry and unmarked. Then, smiling to herself, she got into the driver's seat and, suddenly touched with sick cold, turned around to look. "Why," she said half whispering, "you're not *still* here, you can't be! Why," she said, "I just looked."

"They were strangers in the house," the old woman said.

The skin on the back of Ethel's neck crawled as though some wet thing walked there; the child stared past her, and the old woman's eyes were flat and dead. "What do you want?" Ethel asked, still whispering.

"We got to go back."

"I'll take you." The rain came hard against the windows of the car, and Ethel Sloane, seeing her own hand tremble as she reached for the car key, told herself, don't be afraid, they're not real. "I'll take you," she said, gripping the wheel tight and turning the car to face down the hill. "I'll take you," she said, almost babbling. "I'll take you right back, I promise, see if I don't, I promise I'll take you right back where you want to go."

"He wanted to go home," the old woman said. Her voice was very far away.

"I'll take you, I'll take you." The road was even more slippery than before, and Ethel Sloane told herself, drive carefully, don't be afraid, they're not real. "Right where I found you yesterday, the very spot, I'll take you back."

"They were strangers in the house."

Ethel realized that she was driving faster than she should; she felt the disgusting wet cold coming from the backseat pushing her, forcing her to hurry.

"I'll take you back," she said over and over to the old woman and the child.

"When the strangers are gone, we can go home," the old woman said.

Coming to the last turn before the bridge, the wheels slipped, and, pulling at the steering wheel and shouting, "I'll take you back, I'll take you back," Ethel Sloane could hear only the child's horrible laughter as the car turned and skidded towards the high waters of the creek.

One wheel slipped and spun in the air, and then, wrenching at the car with all her strength, she pulled it back on to the road and stopped.

Crying, breathless, Ethel put her head down on the steering wheel, weak and exhausted. I was almost killed, she told herself, they almost took me with them. She did not need to look into the backseat of the car; the cold was gone, and she knew the seat was dry and empty.

The clerk in the hardware store looked up and, seeing Ethel Sloane, smiled politely and then, looking again, frowned. "You feeling poorly this morning, Mrs. Sloane?" he asked. "Rain bothering you?"

"I almost had an accident on the road," Ethel Sloane said.

"On the old Sanderson road?" The clerk's hands were very still on the counter. "An accident?"

Ethel Sloane opened her mouth and then shut it again. "Yes," she said at last. "The car skidded."

"We don't use that road much," the clerk said. Ethel started to speak, but stopped herself.

"It's got a bad name locally, that road," he said. "What were you needing this morning?"

Ethel thought, and finally said, "Clothespins, I guess I must need clothespins. About the Sanderson road—"

"Yes?" said the clerk, his back to her.

"Nothing," Ethel said.

"Clothespins," the clerk said, putting a box on the counter. "By the way, will you and the mister be coming to the PTA social tomorrow night?"

"We certainly will," said Ethel Sloane.

ONE CHANCE

Ethel Helene Coen

It was the terrible summer of 1720. The plague hung darkly over shuddering New Orleans. Its black wings beat at every door, and there were few that had not opened to its dread presence. Paul had seen his mother, father, sisters, and friends swept down by its mowing sickle. Only Marie remained for him—beautiful Marie with her love for him that he knew was stronger than any plague—the one thing in all the world that was left to sustain him.

"Let us fly from this accursed place," he pleaded. "Let us try to find happiness elsewhere. Neither of us has a tie to bind us here—is not your sister to be buried this very day? Ah, Saint Louis has seen many such scenes in this last month—we will fly to Canada and begin all over."

"But, my darling," she protested, "you forget the quarantine: no one is allowed to enter or leave the city; your plan is hopeless."

"No . . . no . . . I have a plan—such a terrible one that I shudder to think of it. Here it is—"

While he rapidly sketched their one desperate chance, Marie's face blanched, but when he finished, she agreed.

The daughter of the mayor had died that morning. A special dispensation had been secured to ship her body to Charleston for burial. The body rested in its casket in Saint Louis cathedral and was to be shipped by boat that night.

At six o'clock that evening the cathedral was empty save for its silent occupants awaiting burial. The tall wax tapers glimmered fitfully over the scene of desolation. Paul and Marie crept in and went to the casket of the mayor's daughter. Paul rapidly unscrewed the wooden top, removed the slight body, put it into a large sack; and Marie, nearly swooning from terror, got into the coffin.

"Here is a flask of water," Paul whispered, "and remember—not a sound, no matter what happens. I shall sneak aboard the boat before it sails at nine. After we are out for half an hour I will let you out of this. It is our only chance."

"Yes, I know," Marie whispered chokingly. "I shall make no sound . . . now go . . . the priests will soon be back, so one last kiss, until we are on the boat."

He kissed her passionately, then loosely screwed the top on the casket.

Stealing with his awful burden to the yard in the back of the cathedral, he remembered a deep, dried-up well in one corner of the yard. Just the place to dispose of the body.

God rest the poor girl's soul, he thought; she, wherever she is, will understand that I meant no sacrilege to her remains, but this is my one chance of happiness . . . my only chance.

His task ended, he climbed the iron wall and walked rapidly up Pirates Alley and wandered over the Vieux Carré until eight-thirty. Thank God—it was time to try the success of their daring venture. His head whirled and his heart beat like a trip-hammer as he slipped on to the boat unobserved by any but the dock hands, who probably considered him one of their number. He secreted himself in a dark corner and waited. After centuries had passed, or so it seemed to him, the boat started moving. It would not be long now. He did not stop to think what would happen when they were caught—that would take care of itself.

Ah—voices, coming nearer and nearer. From his corner Paul could distinctly see the silhouettes of the two men who were approaching.

"Yes," said one, "it is sad. The mayor is broken-hearted—we were going to take her body to Charleston—but the mayor had her buried from Saint Louis just after the sun went down."

THE FLY

Arthur Porges

Shortly after noon the man unslung his Geiger counter and placed it carefully upon a flat rock by a thick, inviting patch of grass. He listened to the faint, erratic background ticking for a moment, then snapped off the current. No point in running the battery down just to hear stray cosmic rays and residual radioactivity. So far he'd found nothing potent, not a single trace of workable ore.

Squatting, he unpacked an ample lunch of hard-boiled eggs, bread, fruit, and a thermos of black coffee. He ate hungrily, but with the neat, crumbless manners of an outdoorsman; and when the last bite was gone, he stretched out, braced on his elbows, to sip the remaining drops of coffee. It felt mighty good, he thought, to get off your feet after a six-hour hike through rough country.

As he lay there, savoring the strong brew, his gaze suddenly narrowed and became fixed. Right before his eyes, artfully spun between two twigs and a small, mossy boulder, a cunning snare for the unwary spread its threads of wet silver in the network of death. It was the instinctive creation of a master engineer, a nearly perfect logarithmic spiral, stirring gently in a slight updraft.

He studied it curiously, tracing with growing interest the special cable, attached only at the ends, that led from a silk cushion at the web's center up to a crevice in the boulder. He knew that the mistress of this snare must be hidden there, crouching with one hind foot on her primitive telegraph wire and awaiting those welcome vibrations which meant a victim thrashing hopelessly among the sticky threads.

He turned his head and soon found her. Deep in the dark crevice the spider's eyes formed a sinister, jeweled pattern. Yes, she was at home, patiently watchful. It was all very efficient and, in a reflective mood, drowsy from his exertions and a full stomach, he pondered the small miracle before him: how a speck of protoplasm, a mere dot of white nerve tissue which was a spider's brain, had antedated the mind of Euclid by countless centuries. Spiders are an ancient race; ages before man wrought wonders through his subtle abstractions of points and lines, a spiral not to be distinguished from this one winnowed the breezes of some prehistoric summer.

Then he blinked, his attention once more sharpened. A glowing gem, glistening metallic blue, had planted itself squarely upon the web. As if manipulated by a conjurer, the bluebottle fly had appeared from nowhere. It was an exceptionally fine specimen, he decided, large, perfectly formed, and brilliantly rich in hue.

He eyed the insect wonderingly. Where was the usual panic, the frantic struggling, the shrill, terrified buzzing? It rested there with an odd indifference to restraint that puzzled him.

There was at least one reasonable explanation. The fly might be sick or dying, the prey of parasites. Fungi and the ubiquitous roundworms shattered the ranks of even the most fertile. So unnaturally still was this fly that the spider, wholly unaware of its feathery landing, dreamed on in her shaded lair.

Then, as he watched, the bluebottle, stupidly perverse, gave a single sharp tug; its powerful wings blurred momentarily and a high-pitched buzz sounded. The man sighed, almost tempted to interfere. Not that it mattered how soon the fly betrayed itself. Eventually the spider would have made a routine inspection; and unlike most people, he knew her for a staunch friend of man, a tireless killer of insect pests. It was not for him to steal her dinner and tear her web.

But now, silent and swift, a pea on eight hairy, agile legs, she glided over her swaying net. An age-old tragedy was about to be enacted, and the man waited with pitying interest for the inevitable denouement.

About an inch from her prey, the spider paused briefly, estimating the situation with diamond-bright, soulless eyes. The man knew what would follow. Utterly contemptuous of a mere fly, however large, lacking either sting or fangs, the spider would unhesitatingly close in, swathe the insect with silk, and drag it to her nest in the rock, there to be drained at leisure.

But instead of a fearless attack, the spider edged cautiously nearer. She seemed doubtful, even uneasy. The fly's strange passivity apparently worried her. He saw the needle-pointed mandibles working, ludicrously suggestive of a woman wringing her hands in agonized indecision.

Reluctantly she crept forward. In a moment she would turn about, squirt a preliminary jet of silk over the bluebottle, and by dexterously rotating the fly with her hind legs, wrap it in a gleaming shroud. And so it appeared, for satisfied with a closer inspection, she forgot her fears and whirled, thrusting her spinnerets towards the motionless insect.

Then the man saw a startling, an incredible thing. There was a metallic flash as a jointed, shining rod stabbed from the fly's head like some fantastic rapier. It licked out with lightning precision, pierced the spider's plump abdomen, and remained extended, forming a terrible link between them.

He gulped, tense with disbelief. A bluebottle fly, a mere lapper of carrion, with an extensible, sucking proboscis! It was impossible. Its tongue is only an absorbing cushion, designed for sponging up liquids. But then was this really a fly after all? Insects often mimic each other and he was no longer familiar with such points. No, a bluebottle is unmistakable; besides, this was a true fly, two wings and everything. Rusty or not, he knew that much.

The spider had stiffened as the queer lance struck home. Now she was rigid, obviously paralyzed. And her swollen abdomen was contracting like a tiny fist as the fly sucked its juices through that slender, pulsating tube.

He peered more closely, raising himself to his knees and longing for a lens. It seemed to his straining gaze as if that gruesome beak came not from the mouth region at all, but through a minute, hatchlike opening between the faceted eyes, with a nearly invisible square door ajar. But that was absurd; it must be the glare, and—ah! Flickering, the rod retracted; there was definitely no such opening now. Apparently the bright sun was playing tricks. The spider stood shriveled, a pitiful husk, still upright on her thin legs.

One thing was certain, he must have this remarkable fly. If not a new species, it was surely very rare. Fortunately it was stuck fast in the web. Killing the spider could not help it. He knew the steely toughness of those elastic strands, each a tight helix filled with superbly tenacious gum. Very few insects, and those only among the strongest, ever tear free. He gingerly extended his thumb and forefinger. Easy now; he had to pull the fly loose without crushing it.

Then he stopped, almost touching the insect, and staring hard. He was uneasy, a little frightened. A brightly glowing spot, brilliant even in the glaring sunlight, was throbbing on the very tip of the blue abdomen. A reedy, barely audible whine was coming from the trapped insect. He thought momentarily of fireflies, only to dismiss the notion with scorn for his own stupidity. Of course, a firefly is actually a beetle, and this thing was—not that, anyway.

Excited, he reached forward again, but as his plucking fingers approached, the fly rose smoothly in a vertical ascent, lifting a pyramid of taut strands and tearing a gap in the web as easily as a falling stone. The man was alert, however. His cupped hand, nervously swift, snapped over the insect, and he gave a satisfied grunt.

But the captive buzzed in his eager grasp with a furious vitality that appalled him, and he yelped as a searing, slashing pain scalded the sensitive palm. Involuntarily he relaxed his grip. There was a streak of electric blue as his prize soared, glinting in the sun. For an instant he saw that odd glowworm taillight, a dazzling spark against the darker sky, then nothing.

He examined the wound, swearing bitterly. It was purple, and already little blisters were forming. There was no sign of a puncture. Evidently the creature had not used its lancet, but merely spurted venom—acid, perhaps—on the skin. Certainly the injury felt very much like a bad burn. Damn and blast! He'd kicked away a real find, an insect probably new to science. With a little more care he might have caught it.

Stiff and vexed, he got sullenly to his feet and repacked the lunch kit. He reached for the Geiger counter, snapped on the current, took one step towards a distant rocky outcrop—and froze. The slight background noise had given way to a veritable roar, an electronic avalanche that could mean only one thing. He stood there, scrutinizing the grassy knoll and shaking his head in profound mystification. Frowning, he put down the counter. As he withdrew his hand, the frantic chatter quickly faded out. He waited, half-stooped, a blank look in his eyes. Suddenly they lit with doubting, half-fearful comprehension. Catlike, he stalked the clicking instrument, holding one arm outstretched, gradually advancing the blistered palm.

And the Geiger counter raved anew.

TO BUILD A FIRE

Jack London

Day had broken cold and gray, exceedingly cold and gray, when the man turned aside from the main Yukon trail and climbed the high earth bank, where a dim and little-traveled trail led eastward through the fat spruce timberland. It was a steep bank, and he paused for breath at the top, excusing the act to himself by looking at his watch. It was nine o'clock. There was no sun nor hint of sun, though there was not a cloud in the sky. It was a clear day, and yet there seemed an intangible pall over the face of things, a subtle gloom that made the day dark, and that was due to the absence of sun. This fact did not worry the man. He was used to the lack of sun. It had been days since he had seen the sun, and he knew that a few more days must pass before that cheerful orb, due south, would just peep above the sky line and dip immediately from view.

The man flung a look back along the way he had come. The Yukon lay a mile wide and hidden under three feet of ice. On top of this ice were as many feet of snow. It was all pure white, rolling in gentle undulations where the ice jams of the freeze-up had formed. North and south, as far as his eye could see, it was unbroken white, save for a dark hairline that curved and twisted from around the spruce-covered island to the south, and that curved and twisted away into the north, where it disappeared behind another spruce-covered island. This dark hairline was the trail—the main trail—that led south five hundred miles to the Chilkoot Pass, Dyea, and salt water; and that led north seventy miles to Dawson, and still on to the north a thousand miles to Nulato, and finally to St. Michael, on Bering Sea, a thousand miles and half a thousand more.

But all this—the mysterious, far-reaching hairline trail, the absence of sun from the sky, the tremendous cold, and the strangeness and weirdness of it all—made no impression on the man. It was not because he was long used to it. He was a newcomer in the land, a *chechaquo*, and this was his first winter. The trouble with him was that he was without imagination. He was quick and alert in the things of life, but only in the things, and not in the significance. Fifty degrees below zero meant eighty-odd degrees of frost. Such fact impressed him as being cold and uncomfortable, and that was all. It did not lead him to meditate upon his frailty as a creature of temperature, and upon man's frailty in general, able only to live within certain narrow limits of heat and cold; and from there on it did not lead him to the conjectural field of immortality and man's place in the universe. Fifty degrees below zero stood for a bite of frost that hurt and that must be guarded against by the use of mittens, ear flaps, warm moccasins, and thick socks. Fifty degrees below zero was to him just precisely fifty degrees below zero. That there should be anything more to it than that was a thought that never entered his head.

As he turned to go on, he spat speculatively. There was a sharp, explosive crackle that startled him. He spat again. And again, in the air, before it could fall to the snow, the spittle crackled. He knew that at fifty below spittle crackled on the snow, but this spittle had crackled in the air. Undoubtedly it was colder than fifty below—how much colder he did not know. But the temperature did not matter. He was bound for the old claim on the left fork of Henderson Creek, where the boys were already. They had come over across the divide from the Indian Creek country, while he had come the roundabout way to take a look at the possibilities of getting out logs in the spring from the islands in the Yukon. He would be into camp by six o'clock; a bit after dark, it was true, but the boys would be there, a fire would be going, and a hot supper would be ready. As for lunch, he pressed his hand against the protruding bundle under his jacket. It was also under his shirt, wrapped up in a handkerchief and lying against the naked skin. It was the only way to keep the biscuits from freezing. He smiled agreeably to himself as he thought of those biscuits, each cut open and sopped in bacon grease, and each enclosing a generous slice of fried bacon.

He plunged in among the big spruce trees. The trail was faint. A foot of snow had fallen since the last sled had passed over, and he was glad he was without a sled, traveling light. In fact, he carried nothing but the lunch wrapped in the handkerchief. He was surprised, however, at the cold. It certainly was cold, he concluded, as he rubbed his numb nose and cheek-bones with his mittened hand. He was a warm-whiskered man, but the hair on his face did not protect the high cheekbones and the eager nose that thrust itself aggressively into the frosty air.

At the man's heels trotted a dog, a big native husky, the proper wolf dog, gray-coated and without any visible or temperamental difference from its brother the wild wolf. The animal was depressed by the tremendous cold. It knew that it was no time for traveling. Its instinct told it a truer tale than was told to the man by the man's judgment. In reality, it was not merely colder than fifty below zero; it was colder than sixty below, than seventy below. It was seventy-five below zero. Since the freezing point is thirty-two above zero, it meant that one hundred and seven degrees of frost obtained. The dog did not know anything about thermometers. Possibly in its brain there was no sharp consciousness of a condition of very cold such as was in the man's brain. But the brute had its instinct. It experienced a vague but menacing apprehension that subdued it and made it slink along at the man's heels, and that made it question eagerly every unwonted movement of the man as if expecting him to go into camp or to seek shelter somewhere and build a fire. The dog had learned fire, and it wanted fire, or else to burrow under the snow and cuddle its warmth away from the air.

The frozen moisture of its breathing had settled on its fur in a fine powder of frost, and especially were its jowls, muzzle, and eyelashes whitened by its crystaled breath. The man's red beard and mustache were likewise frosted, but more solidly, the deposit taking the form of ice and increasing with every warm, moist breath he exhaled. Also, the man was chewing tobacco, and the muzzle of ice held his lips so rigidly that he was unable to clear his chin when he expelled the juice. The result was that a crystal beard of the color and solidity of amber was increasing its length on his chin. If he fell down it would shatter itself, like glass, into brittle fragments. But he did not mind the appendage. It was the penalty all tobacco chewers paid in that country, and he had been out before in two cold snaps. They had not been so cold as this, he knew, but by the spirit thermometer at Sixty Mile he knew they had been registered at fifty below and at fifty-five.

He held on through the level stretch of woods for several miles, crossed a wide flat of nigger heads, and dropped down a bank to the frozen bed of a small stream. This was Henderson Creek, and he knew he was ten miles from the forks. He looked at his watch. It was ten o'clock. He was making four miles an hour, and he calculated that he would arrive at the forks at half-past twelve. He decided to celebrate that event by eating his lunch there.

The dog dropped in again at his heels, with a tail drooping discouragement, as the man swung along the creek bed. The furrow of the old sled trail was plainly visible, but a dozen inches of snow covered the marks of the last runners. In a month no man had come up or down that silent creek. The man held steadily on. He was not much given to thinking, and just then particularly he had nothing to think about save that he would eat lunch at the forks and that at six o'clock he would be in camp with the boys. There was nobody to talk to; and, had there been, speech would have been impossible because of the ice muzzle on his mouth. So he continued monotonously to chew tobacco and to increase the length of his amber beard.

Once in a while the thought reiterated itself that it was very cold and that he had never experienced such cold. As he walked along he rubbed his cheekbones and nose with the back of his mittened hand. He did this automatically, now and again changing hands. But, rub as he would, the instant he stopped his cheekbones went numb, and the following instant the end of his nose went numb. He was sure to frost his cheeks; he knew that, and experienced a pang of regret that he had not devised a nose strap of the sort Bud wore in cold snaps. Such a strap passed across the cheeks, as well, and saved them. But it didn't matter much, after all. What were frosted cheeks? A bit painful, that was all; they were never serious.

Empty as the man's mind was of thoughts, he was keenly observant, and he noticed the changes in the creek, the curves and bends and timber jams, and always he sharply noted where he placed his feet. Once, coming around a bend, he shied abruptly, like a startled horse, curved away from the place where he had been walking, and retreated several paces back along the trail. The creek he knew was frozen clear to the bottom—no creek could contain water in that arctic winter—but he knew also that there were springs that bubbled out from the hillsides and ran along under the snow and on top [of] the ice of the creek. He knew that the coldest snaps never froze these springs, and he knew likewise their danger. They were traps. They hid pools of water under the snow that might be three inches deep, or three feet. Sometimes a skin of ice half an inch thick covered them, and in turn was covered by the snow. Sometimes there were alternate layers of water and ice skin, so that when one broke through he kept on breaking through for a while, sometimes wetting himself to the waist.

That was why he had shied in such panic. He had felt the give under his feet and heard the crackle of a snow-hidden ice skin. And to get his feet wet in such a temperature meant trouble and danger. At the very least it meant delay, for he would be forced to stop and build a fire, and under its protection to bare his feet while he dried his socks and moccasins. He stood and studied the creek bed and its banks, and decided that the flow of water came from the right. He reflected awhile, rubbing his nose and cheeks, then skirted to the left, stepping gingerly and testing the footing for each step. Once clear of the danger, he took a fresh chew of tobacco and swung along at his four-mile gait.

In the course of the next two hours he came upon several similar traps. Usually the snow above the hidden pools had a sunken, candied appearance that advertised the danger. Once again, however, he had a close call; and once, suspecting danger, he compelled the dog to go on in front. The dog did not want to go. It hung back until the man shoved it forward, and then it went quickly across the white, unbroken surface. Suddenly it broke through, floundered to one side, and got away to firmer footing. It had wet its forefeet and legs, and almost immediately the water that clung to it turned to ice. It made quick efforts to lick the ice off its legs, then dropped down in the snow and began to bite out the ice that had formed between the toes. This was a matter of instinct. To permit the ice to remain would mean sore feet. It did not know this. It merely obeyed the mysterious prompting that arose from the deep crypts of its being. But the man knew, having achieved a judgment on the subject, and he removed the mitten from his right hand and helped tear out the ice particles. He did not expose his fingers more than a minute, and was astonished at the swift numbness that smote them. It certainly was cold. He pulled on the mitten hastily, and beat the hand savagely across his chest.

At twelve o'clock the day was at its brightest. Yet the sun was too far south on its winter journey to clear the horizon. The bulge of the earth intervened between it and Henderson Creek, where the man walked under a clear sky at noon and cast no shadow. At half-past twelve, to the minute, he arrived at the forks of the creek. He was pleased at the speed he had made. If he kept it up, he would certainly be with the boys by six. He unbuttoned his jacket and shirt and drew forth his lunch. The action consumed no more than a quarter of a minute, yet in that brief moment the numbness laid hold of the exposed fingers. He did not put the mitten on, but, instead, struck the fingers a dozen sharp smashes against his leg. Then he sat down on a snow-covered log to eat. The sting that followed upon the striking of his fingers against his leg ceased so quickly that he was startled. He had had no chance to take a bite of biscuit. He struck the fingers repeatedly and returned them to the mitten, baring the other hand for the purpose of eating. He tried to take a mouthful, but the ice muzzle prevented. He had forgotten to build a fire and thaw out. He chuckled at his foolishness and as he chuckled he noted the numbness creeping into the exposed fingers. Also, he noted that the stinging which had first come to his toes when he sat down was already passing away. He wondered whether the toes were warm or numb. He moved them inside the moccasins and decided that they were numb.

He pulled the mitten on hurriedly and stood up. He was a bit frightened. He stamped up and down until the stinging returned into the feet. It certainly was cold, was his thought. That man from Sulphur Creek had spoken the truth when telling how cold it sometimes got in the country. And he had laughed at him at the time! That showed one must not be too sure of things. There was no mistake about it, it was cold. He strode up and down, stamping his feet and threshing his arms, until reassured by the returning warmth. Then he got out matches and proceeded to make a fire. From the undergrowth, where high water of the previous spring had lodged a supply of seasoned twigs, he got his firewood. Working carefully from a small beginning, he soon had a roaring fire, over which he thawed the ice from his face and in the protection of which he ate his biscuits. For the moment the cold of space was outwitted. The dog took satisfaction in the fire, stretching out close enough for warmth and far enough away to escape being singed.

When the man had finished, he filled his pipe and took his comfortable time over a smoke. Then he pulled on his mittens, settled the ear flaps of his cap firmly about his ears, and took the creek trail up the left fork. The dog was disappointed and yearned back toward the fire. This man did not know cold. Possibly all the generations of his ancestry had been ignorant of cold, of real cold, of cold one hundred and seven degrees below freezing point. But the dog knew; all its ancestry knew, and it had inherited the knowledge. And it knew that it was not good to walk abroad in such fearful cold. It was the time to lie snug in a hole in the snow and wait for a curtain of cloud to be drawn across the face of outer space whence this cold came. On the other hand, there was no keen intimacy between the dog and the man. The one was the toll slave of the other, and the only caresses it had ever received were the caresses of the whip-lash and of harsh and menacing throat sounds that threatened the whiplash. So the dog made no effort to communicate its apprehension to the man. It was not concerned in the welfare of the man; it was for its own sake that it yearned back toward the fire. But the man whistled, and spoke to it with the sound of whiplashes, and the dog swung in at the man's heels and followed after.

The man took a chew of tobacco and proceeded to start a new amber beard. Also, his moist breath quickly powdered with white his mustache, eyebrows, and lashes. There did not seem to be so many springs on the left fork of the Henderson, and for half an hour the man saw no signs of any. And then it happened. At a place where there were no signs, where the soft, unbroken snow seemed to advertise solidity beneath, the man broke through. It was not deep. He wet himself halfway to the knees before he floundered out to the firm crust.

He was angry, and cursed his luck aloud. He had hoped to get into camp with the boys at six o'clock, and this would delay him an hour, for he would have to build a fire and dry out his footgear. This was imperative at that low temperature—he knew that much; and he turned aside to the bank, which he climbed. On top, tangled in the underbrush about the trunks of several small spruce trees, was a high-water deposit of dry firewood—sticks and twigs, principally, but also larger portions of seasoned branches and fine, dry, last year's grasses. He threw down several large pieces on top of the snow. This served for a foundation and prevented the young flame from drowning itself in the snow it otherwise would melt. The flame he got by touching a match to a small shred of birch bark that he took from his pocket. This burned even more readily than paper. Placing it on the foundation, he fed the young flame with wisps of dry grass and with the tiniest dry twigs.

He worked slowly and carefully, keenly aware of his danger. Gradually, as the flame grew stronger, he increased the size of the twigs with which he fed it. He squatted in the snow, pulling the twigs out from their entanglement in the brush and feeding directly to the flame. He knew there must be no failure. When it is seventy-five below zero, a man must not fail in his first attempt to build a fire—that is, if his feet are wet. If his feet are dry, and he fails, he can run along the trail for half a mile and restore his circulation. But the circulation of wet and freezing feet cannot be restored by running when it is seventy-five below. No matter how fast he runs, the wet feet will freeze the harder.

All this the man knew. The old-timer on Sulphur Creek had told him about it the previous fall, and now he was appreciating the advice. Already all sensation had gone out of his feet. To build the fire he had been forced to remove his mittens, and the fingers had quickly gone numb. His pace of four miles an hour had kept his heart pumping blood to the surface of his body and to all the extremities. But the instant he stopped, the action of the pump eased down. The cold of space smote the unprotected tip of the planet, and he, being on that unprotected tip, received the full force of the blow. The blood of his body recoiled before it. The blood was alive, like the dog, and like the dog it wanted to hide away and cover itself up from the fearful cold. So long as he walked four miles an hour, he pumped that blood, willy-nilly, to the surface; but now it ebbed away and sank down into the recesses of his body. The extremities were the first to feel its absence. His wet feet froze the faster, and his exposed fingers numbed the faster, though they had not yet begun to freeze. Nose and cheeks were already freezing, while the skin of all his body chilled as it lost its blood.

But he was safe. Toes and nose and cheeks would be only touched by the frost, for the fire was beginning to burn with strength. He was feeding it with twigs the size of his finger. In another minute he would be able to feed it with branches the size of his wrist, and then he could remove his wet footgear, and, while it dried, he could keep his naked feet warm by the fire, rubbing them at first, of course, with snow. The fire was a success. He was safe. He remembered the advice of the old-timer on Sulphur Creek, and smiled. The old-timer had been very serious in laying down the law that no man must travel alone in the Klondike after fifty below. Well, here he was; he had had the accident; he was alone; and he had saved himself. Those old-timers were rather womanish, some of them, he thought. All a man had to do was to keep his head, and he was all right. Any man who was a man could travel alone. But it was surprising, the rapidity with which his cheeks and nose were freezing. And he had not thought his fingers could go lifeless in so short a time. Lifeless they were, for he could scarcely make them move together to grip a twig, and they seemed remote from his body and from him. When he touched a twig, he had to look and see whether or not he had hold of it. The wires were pretty well down between him and his finger ends.

All of which counted for little. There was the fire, snapping and crackling and promising life with every dancing flame. He started to untie his moccasins. They were coated with ice; the thick German socks were like sheaths of iron halfway to the knees; and the moccasin strings were like rods of steel all twisted and knotted as by some conflagration. For a moment he tugged with his numb fingers, then, realizing the folly of it, he drew his sheath knife.

But before he could cut the strings, it happened. It was his own fault or, rather, his mistake. He should not have built the fire under the spruce tree. He should have built it in the open. But it had been easier to pull the twigs from the brush and drop them directly on the fire. Now the tree under which he had done this carried a weight of snow on its boughs. No wind had blown for weeks, and each bough was fully freighted. Each time he had pulled a twig he had communicated a slight agitation to the tree—an imperceptible agitation, so far as he was concerned, but an agitation sufficient to bring about the disaster. High up in the tree one bough capsized its load of snow. This fell on the boughs beneath, capsizing them. This process continued, spreading out and involving the whole tree. It grew like an avalanche, and it descended without warning upon the man and the fire, and the fire was blotted out! Where it had burned was a mantle of fresh and disordered snow.

The man was shocked. It was as though he had just heard his own sentence of death. For a moment he sat and stared at the spot where the fire had been. Then he grew very calm. Perhaps the old-timer on Sulphur Creek was right. If he had only had a trail mate he would have been in no danger now. The trail mate could have built the fire. Well, it was up to him to build the fire over again, and this second time there must be no failure. Even if he succeeded, he would most likely lose some toes. His feet must be badly frozen by now, and there would be some time before the second fire was ready.

Such were his thoughts, but he did not sit and think them. He was busy all the time they were passing through his mind. He made a new foundation for a fire, this time in the open, where no treacherous tree could blot it out. Next he gathered dry grasses and tiny twigs from the high-water flotsam. He could not bring his fingers together to pull them out, but he was able to gather them by the handful. In this way he got many rotten twigs and bits of green moss that were undesirable, but it was the best he could do. He worked methodically, even collecting an armful of the larger branches to be used later when the fire gathered strength. And all the while the dog sat and watched him, a certain yearning wistfulness in its eyes, for it looked upon him as the fire provider, and the fire was slow in coming.

When all was ready, the man reached in his pocket for a second piece of birch bark. He knew the bark was there, and, though he could not feel it with his fingers, he could hear its crisp rustling as he fumbled for it. Try as he would, he could not clutch hold of it. And all the time, in his consciousness, was the knowledge that each instant his feet were freezing. This thought tended to put him in a panic, but he fought against it and kept calm. He pulled on his mittens with his teeth, and threshed his arms back and forth, beating his hands with all his might against his sides. He did this sitting down, and he stood up to do it; and all the while the dog sat in the snow, its wolf brush of a tail curled around warmly over its forefeet, its sharp wolf ears pricked forward intently as it watched the man. And the man, as he beat and threshed with his arms and hands, felt a great surge of envy as he regarded the creature that was warm and secure in its natural covering.

After a time he was aware of the first faraway signals of sensation in his beaten fingers. The faint tingling grew stronger till it evolved into a stinging ache that was excruciating, but which the man hailed with satisfaction. He stripped the mitten from his right hand and fetched forth the birch bark. The exposed fingers were quickly going numb again. Next he brought out his bunch of sulphur matches. But the tremendous cold had already driven the life out of his fingers. In his effort to separate one match from the others, the whole bunch fell in the snow. He tried to pick it out of the snow, but failed. The dead fingers could neither touch nor clutch. He was very careful. He drove the thought of his freezing feet, and nose, and cheeks, out of his mind, devoting his whole soul to the matches. He watched, using the sense of vision in place of that of touch, and when he saw his fingers on each side the bunch, he closed them—that is, he willed to close them, for the wires were down, and the fingers did not obey. He pulled the mitten on the right hand, and beat it fiercely against his knee. Then, with both mittened hands, he scooped the bunch of matches, along with much snow, into his lap. Yet he was no better off.

After some manipulation he managed to get the bunch between the heels of his mittened hands. In this fashion he carried it to his mouth. The ice crackled and snapped when by a violent effort he opened his mouth. He drew the lower jaw in, curled the upper lip out of the way, and scraped the bunch with his upper teeth in order to separate a match. He succeeded in getting one, which he dropped on his lap. He was no better off. He could not pick it up. Then he devised a way. He picked it up in his teeth and scratched it on his leg. Twenty times he scratched before he succeeded in lighting it. As it flamed he held it with his teeth to the birch bark. But the burning brimstone went up his nostrils and into his lungs, causing him to cough spasmodically. The match fell into the snow and went out.

The old-timer on Sulphur Creek was right, he thought in the moment of controlled despair that ensued: after fifty below, a man should travel with a partner. He beat his hands, but failed in exciting any sensation. Suddenly he bared both hands, removing the mittens with his teeth. He caught the whole bunch between the heels of his hands. His arm muscles not being frozen enabled him to press the hand heels tightly against the matches. Then he scratched the bunch along his leg. It flared into flame, seventy sulphur matches at once! There was no wind to blow them out. He kept his head to one side to escape the strangling fumes, and held the blazing bunch to the birch bark. As he so held it, he became aware of sensation in his hand. His flesh was burning. He could smell it. Deep down below the surface he could feel it. The sensation developed into pain that grew acute. And still he endured it, holding the flame of the matches clumsily to the bark that would not light readily because his own burning hands were in the way, absorbing most of the flame.

At last, when he could endure no more, he jerked his hands apart. The blazing matches fell sizzling into the snow, but the birch bark was alight. He began laying dry grasses and the tiniest twigs on the flame. He could not pick and choose, for he had to lift the fuel between the heels of his hands. Small pieces of rotten wood and green moss clung to the twigs, and he bit them off as well as he could with his teeth. He cherished the flame carefully and awkwardly. It meant life, and it must not perish. The withdrawal of blood from the surface of his body now made him begin to shiver, and he grew more awkward. A large piece of green moss fell squarely on the little fire. He tried to poke it out with his fingers but his shivering frame made him poke too far, and he disrupted the nucleus of the little fire, the burning grass and tiny twigs separating and scattering. He tried to poke them together again, but in spite of the tenseness of the effort, his shivering got away with him, and the twigs were hopelessly scattered. Each twig gushed a puff of smoke and went out. The fire provider had failed. As he looked apathetically about him, his eyes chanced on the dog, sitting across the ruins of the fire from him, in the snow, making restless, hunching movements, slightly lifting one forefoot and then the other, shifting its weight back and forth on them with wistful eagerness.

The sight of the dog put a wild idea into his head. He remembered the tale of the man, caught in a blizzard, who killed a steer and crawled inside the carcass, and so was saved.

He would kill the dog and bury his hands in the warm body until the numbness went out of them. Then he could build another fire. He spoke to the dog, calling it to him; but in his voice was a strange note of fear that frightened the animal, who had never known the man to speak in such way before. Something was the matter, and its suspicious nature sensed danger—it knew not what danger, but somewhere, somehow, in its brain arose an apprehension of the man. It flattened its ears down at the sound of the man's voice, and its restless, hunching movements and the lifting and shifting of its forefeet became more pronounced; but it would not come to the man. He got on his hands and knees and crawled toward the dog. This unusual posture again excited suspicion, and the animal sidled mincingly away.

The man sat up in the snow for a moment and struggled for calmness. Then he pulled on his mittens, by means of his teeth, and got upon his feet. He glanced down at first in order to assure himself that he was really standing up, for the absence of sensation in his feet left him unrelated to the earth. His erect position in itself started to drive the webs of suspicion from the dog's mind; and when he spoke peremptorily, with the sound of whiplashes in his voice, the dog rendered its customary allegiance and came to him. As it came within reaching distance, the man lost his control. His arms flashed out to the dog, and he experienced genuine surprise when he discovered that his hands could not clutch, that there was neither bend nor feeling in the fingers. He had forgotten for the moment that they were frozen and that they were freezing more and more. All this happened quickly, and before the animal could get away, he encircled its body with his arms. He sat down in the snow, and in this fashion held the dog, while it snarled and whined and struggled.

But it was all he could do, hold its body encircled in his arms and sit there. He realized that he could not kill the dog. There was no way to do it. With his helpless hands he could neither draw nor hold his sheath knife nor throttle the animal. He released it, and it plunged wildly away, with tail between its legs, and still snarling. It halted forty feet away and surveyed him curiously, with ears sharply pricked forward.

The man looked down at his hands in order to locate them, and found them hanging on the ends of his arms. It struck him as curious that one should have to use his eyes in order to find out where his hands were. He began threshing his arms back and forth, beating the mittened hands against his sides. He did this for five minutes, violently, and his heart pumped enough blood up to the surface to put a stop to his shivering. But no sensation was aroused in the hands. He had an impression that they hung like weights on the ends of his arms, but when he tried to run the impression down, he could not find it.

A certain fear of death, dull and oppressive, came to him. This fear quickly became poignant as he realized that it was no longer a mere matter of freezing his fingers and toes, or of losing his hands and feet, but that it was a matter of life and death with the chances against him. This threw him into a panic, and he turned and ran up the creek bed along the old, dim trail. The dog joined in behind and kept up with him. He ran blindly, without intention, in fear such as he had never known in his life. Slowly, as he plowed and floundered through the snow, he began to see things again—the banks of the creek, the old timber jams, the leafless aspens, and the sky. The running made him feel better. He did not shiver. Maybe, if he ran on, his feet would thaw out; and, anyway, if he ran far enough, he would reach camp and the boys. Without doubt he would lose some fingers and toes and some of his face; but the boys would take care of him, and save the rest of him when he got there. And at the same time there was another thought in his mind that said he would never get to the camp and the boys; that it was too many miles away, that the freezing had too great a start on him, and that he would soon be stiff and dead. This thought he kept in the background and refused to consider. Sometimes it pushed itself forward and demanded to be heard, but he thrust it back and strove to think of other things.

It struck him as curious that he could run at all on feet so frozen that he could not feel them when they struck the earth and took the weight of his body. He seemed to himself to skim along above the surface, and to have no connection with the earth. Somewhere he had once seen a winged Mercury, and he wondered if Mercury felt as he felt when skimming over the earth.

His theory of running until he reached camp and the boys had one flaw in it: he lacked the endurance. Several times he stumbled, and finally he tottered, crumpled up, and fell. When he tried to rise, he failed. He must sit and rest, he decided, and next time he would merely walk and keep on going. As he sat and regained his breath, he noted that he was feeling quite warm and comfortable. He was not shivering, and it even seemed that a warm glow had come to his chest and trunk. And yet, when he touched his nose or cheeks, there was no sensation. Running would not thaw them out. Nor would it thaw out his hands and feet. Then the thought came to him that the frozen portions of his body must be extending. He tried to keep this thought down, to forget it, to think of something else; he was aware of the panicky feeling that it caused, and he was afraid of the panic. But the thought asserted itself, and persisted, until it produced a vision of his body totally frozen. This was too much, and he made another wild run along the trail. Once he slowed down to a walk, but the thought of the freezing extending itself made him run again.

And all the time the dog ran with him, at his heels. When he fell down a second time, it curled its tail over its forefeet and sat in front of him, facing him, curiously eager and intent. The warmth and security of the animal angered him, and he cursed it till it flattened down its ears appeasingly. This time the shivering came more quickly upon the man. He was losing in his battle with the frost. It was creeping into his body from all sides. The thought of it drove him on, but he ran no more than a hundred feet, when he staggered and pitched headlong. It was his last panic. When he had recovered his breath and control, he sat up and entertained in his mind the conception of meeting death with dignity. However, the conception did not come to him in such terms. His idea of it was that he had been making a fool of himself, running around like a chicken with its head cut off— such was the simile that occurred to him. Well, he was bound to freeze anyway, and he might as well take it decently. With this newfound peace of mind came the first glimmerings of drowsiness. A good idea, he thought, to sleep off to death. It was like taking an anesthetic. Freezing was not so bad as people thought. There were lots worse ways to die.

He pictured the boys finding his body next day. Suddenly he found himself with them, coming along the trail and looking for himself. And, still with them, he came around a turn in the trail and found himself lying in the snow. He did not belong with himself any more, for even then he was out of himself, standing with the boys and looking at himself in the snow. It certainly was cold, was his thought. When he got back to the States he could tell the folks what real cold was. He drifted on from this to a vision of the old-timer on Sulphur Creek. He could see him quite clearly, warm and comfortable, and smoking a pipe.

"You were right, old hoss; you were right," the man mumbled to the old-timer of Sulphur Creek.

Then the man drowsed off into what seemed to him the most comfortable and satisfying sleep he had ever known. The dog sat facing him and waiting. The brief day drew to a close in a long, slow twilight. There were no signs of a fire to be made, and, besides, never in the dog's experience had it known a man to sit like that in the snow and make no fire. As the twilight drew on, its eager yearning for the fire mastered it, and with a great lifting and shifting of forefeet, it whined softly, then flattened its ears down in anticipation of being chidden by the man. But the man remained silent. Later the dog whined loudly. And still later it crept close to the man and caught the scent of death. This made the animal bristle and back away. A little longer it delayed, howling under the stars that leaped and danced and shone brightly in the cold sky. Then it turned and trotted up the trail in the direction of the camp it knew, where were the other food providers and fire providers.

ACKNOWLEDGMENTS

Excerpt from "Faces at the Window" (pp. 115–25) from *A Little House Sampler* by Laura Ingalls Wilder and Rose Wilder Lane and edited by William T. Anderson. Copyright © 1988 by HarperCollins Publishers, Inc. Reprinted by permission of HarperCollins Publishers.

"He Walked by Day" was originally published in *Weird Tales,* June 1934. Copyright © 1934 by the Popular Fiction Publishing Co., Inc. Reprinted by permission of *Weird Tales* magazine.

"The Wendigo" from *Scary Stories to Tell in the Dark* by Alvin Schwartz. Text copyright © 1981 by Alvin Schwartz. Used by permission of HarperCollins Publishers.

"The Severed Hand" from *Passion and Poison* by Janice M. Del Negro. Published by Marshall Cavendish Children's Books (August 2007) and reprinted with their permission.

"Knock, Knock, Who's There?" from *Cajun Folk Tales* by J. J. Reneaux. Copyright © 1992 by J. J. Reneaux. Published by August House

ABOUT THE EDITOR

Amy Kelley Hoitsma grew up in a family of five girls in Madison, Wisconsin, where summer days were spent at the neighborhood pool and family vacations were spent camping. Rather than a serene wilderness experience, they were a rowdy family affair, where telling stories around the campfire played an important role.

Today she lives in Bozeman, Montana, with her husband and cat, working primarily as a freelance graphic designer. She gets outside to ski, bike, hike, and camp out at every opportunity.